ALSO BY

ERIC-EMMANUEL SCHMITT

The Most Beautiful Book in the World
The Woman with the Bouquet

CONCERTO
TO THE MEMORY
OF AN ANGEL

Eric-Emmanuel Schmitt

CONCERTO TO THE MEMORY OF AN ANGEL

*Translated from the French
by Alison Anderson*

Europa
editions

Europa Editions
116 East 16th Street
New York, N.Y. 10003
www.europaeditions.com
info@europaeditions.com

This work has been published thanks to the support from the
French Ministry of Culture – Centre National du Livre
Ouvrage publié avec le concours du
Ministère français chargé de la Culture – Centre National du Livre

Library of Congress Cataloging in Publication Data is available
ISBN 978-1-60945-009-0

Schmitt, Eric-Emmanuel
Concerto to the Memory of an Angel

Book design by Emanuele Ragnisco
www.mekkanografici.com
Cover illustration by Marcelino Truong

Prepress by Grafica Punto Print – Rome

Printed in Canada

CONTENTS

THE MURDERESS - 9

THE RETURN - 47

CONCERTO TO THE MEMORY OF AN ANGEL - 67

LOVE AT THE ELYSÉE PALACE - 117

A WRITER'S LOGBOOK - 165

ABOUT THE AUTHOR - 185

THE MURDERESS

L ook out, here she comes, the murderess!"

The group of children stopped suddenly in their tracks, like a hand closing. They ran to take refuge at the far end of the washhouse, under the stone bench, a cool, shady spot that would allow them to see without being seen; and now, just to scare themselves further, they held their breath.

Marie Maurestier crossed the street under the noonday sun. She was a tall woman, seventy years of age, slow, stiff, wrinkled, neat about her person, and frequently irritable. Crisp in a black suit cinched tight around her waist, she took mincing steps, either because she feared the heat, or because her inflamed joints made it difficult to walk. She swayed from side to side with an awkward majesty that made her all the more impressive.

The children murmured, "Do you think she's seen us?"

"Come on, let's shout to scare her!"

"Don't be stupid. She's not afraid of anyone or anything. You're the one who ought to panic."

"I'm not afraid."

"If you do something she doesn't like, she'll do you in! Like the others."

"I'm not afraid, I said . . . "

"Sure, like her husbands were stronger and tougher than you are."

"Go on! I'm not scared . . . "

Sensibly, they let Marie Maurestier go by, avoiding any rude remarks or bad jokes.

Twenty years earlier, after two trials, the court had dismissed the case for lack of evidence and released Marie Maurestier from the prison where she had been held in custody. In Saint-Sorlin the majority of villagers believed Marie Maurestier was innocent, except for the children, who would rather cross paths with a murderess any day—it added danger and wonder to their lives. Still, the reason the adults gave for Marie Maurestier's innocence was hardly more rational: they refused to believe they could possibly have an assassin roaming free in their midst: how could they say hello, or share their streets, their shops, and their church with a killer? If they were to preserve their tranquility, she must be just as honest as they were.

No one really liked her, because she was a proud, reserved woman, known to make scathing remarks, and she aroused neither sympathy nor affection. But everyone enjoyed the notoriety she had brought to their town. "The Poisoner of Saint-Sorlin," "The Devil of the Bugey," "The Messalina of Saint-Sorlin-en-Bugey": for a few seasons, these sensational titles had provided the headlines for all the newspapers and radio and television programs. All the fuss attracted curious onlookers, and although people knew their interest was unhealthy, Saint-Sorlin had become front page news. This sudden renown had even incited motorists to leave the autoroute in order to come into town and stop for a drink at the café, or have a bite at the inn, or buy some bread at the boulangerie, where they could casually leaf through a newspaper while hoping to catch a glimpse of Marie Maurestier. Such a pretty peaceful village, with its washhouses gathering water from the springs, their stone walls covered on fine summer days with thousands of roses or eglantines, this little settlement snuggled along a branch of the Rhone where trout and pike swam in abundance—how could it possibly be home to such a dark soul? What a paradoxical form of publicity! If this tiny town of a thousand inhabitants had had a tourist office, they could hardly have found better than Marie Maurestier for their self-promotion; hadn't the mayor, delighted with the crowds of tourists, declared to Marie Maurestier one day in a burst of enthusiasm that he was her "number one fan?" No need to point out that the lady had quickly made short shrift of his fervor with a chilly gaze and hostile silence.

With her wicker basket on her arm, Marie Maurestier walked by the inn without looking inside because she knew that customers were pressing their noses against the little green windowpanes to take a good look at her.

"There's the murderess!"

"Doesn't she look stuck up . . . "

"Snootier than a chamberpot!"

"When you think there are men who died for that!"

"But her name was cleared . . . "

"You can only be cleared if you've done some dark deed, my dear! I was trying to worm some information out of the innkeeper a while ago and he said there's never smoke without fire . . . "

So while the inhabitants may have acquitted her, they let some uncertainty linger, because they weren't about to discourage their visitors by depriving them of this attraction. They were more than willing, while remaining discreet, to show their visitors the path that Marie Maurestier took to go home, or tell them how she spent her time and what her habits were, or point out her house at the top of the ridge . . . And when someone asked if they thought she was guilty, they would reply with a cautious "Who knows?"

Moreover, they were not the only ones who fueled the mystery: television programs regularly debated her fate, emphasizing the ambiguity and the gray areas; and although journalists were obliged to report the court's decision—otherwise Marie

Maurestier's lawyer would force them to pay a stiff fine—they hinted that the dismissal was founded more on a "lack of sufficient evidence" than on proof of innocence.

Thirty feet further along, outside the decorator's shop, Marie Maurestier paused to see whether her worst enemy was there. And he was: Raymond Poussin, with his back to the shop window, samples of fabric in his hand, was holding forth for the benefit of a couple who had entrusted him with an armchair for reupholstering.

"That wretch is as fat as the tow he stuffs his chair backs with and as ugly as the horsehair he uses," she grumbled. She could not hear what he was saying, but she stared hard at him and focused her hatred at the back of his neck.

"La Maurestier, you say? The greatest unpunished criminal in France. Three times over she married men who were richer and older than her. Three times they died only a few years after the wedding. Most unlucky, don't you think? And three times she inherited! Naturally, why should she change her good habits? But with the third one, Georges Jardin, a friend of mine, the suspicions of his five children triggered an inquiry: their father had been in perfect health but no sooner did he marry that monster than he began to decline, then he took to his bed, and two weeks before he died he disinherited the children in favor of that interloper. That was too much! The gendarmes dug up the corpses of the first two husbands, and the experts found suspicious traces of arsenic. They put her in jail while waiting for the trial but it was already too late both for the dead men and for the money. And what do you think she'd done with her fortune, the merry widow? She'd spent it all on a lover, Rudy, or Johnny, or Eddy, something like that, a Yank sort of name. Well, this last one was a young fellow for a change—not an old wreck like the previous ones—and he was good-looking, a surfer from Biarritz who used up all her money on clothes and cars and gambling. A right gigolo he was, a thug, an oyster has more brains. Well, let's not hold it against him, at least he was able to take back what she had nicked from the others. So you're about to tell me there is justice in the world after all? Not at all! She did him in too, the playboy. Not for his money, but because he dumped her. He was never seen again. Maurestier swears he went abroad. If you want my opinion, his corpse is rotting at the bottom of the ocean with a stone around his feet. Only one person must have known about the crimes she committed, and that was her sister Blanche. A simple sort of girl, pretty, and Marie Maurestier, her older sister, had always protected her. Which goes to show that even human trash can have sincere feelings, just like flowers growing out of a pile of dung. Yes, except that the sister died too! In the middle of the trial. Well in this case, obviously, they couldn't pin it on Maurestier because she was already in custody when her sister kicked the bucket, and besides it was in a plane crash that reduced one hundred and thirty-two passengers to ash in a second. The perfect alibi . . . damn lucky, all the same! It would seem there is a God who looks after villains! You see, as soon as her sister, the silly goose—she used to contradict herself the moment she was interrogated, so sometimes she was a witness for the prosecution, and sometimes for the defense—as soon as she disappeared, Maurestier and her lawyer began to feel more relaxed, things were looking good, and they found ways to put things so that the diabolical woman would be let off."

Even from out in the street Marie Maurestier could tell from his reddening face and chaotic gestures that Raymond Poussin was talking about her. The customers were fascinated by the whole business and had not noticed that the woman they were talking about was right there behind them, behind this prosecutor who was vituperating against her.

"She didn't half put her sister's death to good use, did she now, that Maurestier woman! She wept like a fountain and kept saying that it was a good thing after all her younger sister died in that horrible plane crash, otherwise they would have accused her of killing her, too. Everyone thought she killed the people she loved—her husbands, her sister; even when there was no corpse they pinned it on her, the murder of Rudy, Johnny, Eddy—sounds like some rock musician—her so-called lover, whereas in fact the man had gone abroad in order to flee all the debts he'd run up and those bad business ventures of his, all the creditors were on his tail. They conducted the investigation with an eye to prosecution, they wanted to prove she was a criminal no matter what. That was the line her lawyer took and it paid off. Analyses proved that in the cemeteries in the region they used a weed killer that contained arsenic, and consequently any corpse that was disinterred after a few years had gone by would look as if it had been poisoned, particularly if it had rained a lot. She and her lawyer won both her trials. And mind my words, my good people, I do mean she and her lawyer. Neither truth nor justice was served."

Just then, the craftsman felt a sharp pain in the back of his neck. He raised his hand to it, fearful it might be an insect bite, then he turned around.

Marie Maurestier was glaring at him. The old man's heart started to pound wildly, and he could scarcely breathe.

They stared at each other for a few seconds; her gaze was hard, his was panicky. Raymond Poussin had always felt violent emotions whenever he was anywhere near the woman; in the old days he supposed it was love, so much so that he did try to woo her; nowadays he knew it was hatred.

After a good minute had gone by, Marie Maurestier decided to curtail the exchange of gazes with a shrug of her shoulders, and she went on her way as if nothing had happened.

Staid, upright, she walked past the terrace of the café where her appearance brought a temporary halt to conversations, then she entered the butcher's shop.

There, too, people stopped talking. Modestly, she joined the line behind the other customers until the boss, in what seemed like obedience to a tacit agreement, put aside the order he was preparing to indicate that he would serve her before the others.

No one protested. Not only did people accept that Marie Maurestier was granted a special status, they also became thoughtful, painfully thoughtful, the moment they found themselves in her presence. As they no longer dared converse in front of her, or even speak to her, her legend having so greatly surpassed her individual person, they waited for her to leave as soon as possible.

Why could no one forget her? Why, even when her name had been cleared, had she become a myth? Why did everyone still take such an interest in her case ten, twenty years later?

Because Marie Maurestier was in possession of that vital ambiguity that makes the public pause for thought, that duality that is the making of a star: her physical appearance did not coincide with her behavior. In everyday life, a nurse who marries one of her rich, elderly patients is generally a pretty, charming girl, who emphasizes her ample curves— in all the right places—by wearing sexy outfits. Marie Maurestier, however, even when she was young, had never looked young: her body seemed withered, as if she'd gone through menopause before her time; she was an ungainly horse with a gloomy face, who wore severe clothing—shirts with high collars, enormous glasses, shoes more sturdy than glamorous. This woman whom the gossip columnists described as a man-eater looked like nothing so much as a woman who knew nothing of desire or sexuality. What possible connection could there be between her virtuous features and her multiple marriages or her passion for Rudy, the tousle-haired lover, smoker of joints, sportsman with his shirt unbuttoned on his suntanned chest? Another contradiction: in the eyes of the common folk, a murderer who uses poison, in particular a murderer who's done it more than once, must have sharp, pointed features signaling vice, vengeance, and nastiness; but Marie Maurestier had more of the scrupulous schoolmarm about her, or even—she was very pious, and made a great show of her faith—a catechism teacher. In short, no matter what people said about her, her physical aspect never coincided: it matched neither her love affairs nor her crimes.

"There's no reason why I should go before everyone else," murmured Marie Maurestier in a humble, moist voice, as if she were being granted this privilege for the first time.

"I do as I like in my own shop, Madame Maurestier," answered the butcher, calmly. "These ladies and gentlemen don't mind, now, do they?"

The customers shook their heads.

"Well then, some calf's liver for me and some lung for my cat."

The customers could not help but listen to her order as if it might be the formula for some sort of poison.

Was the problem not simply that Marie Maurestier looked inoffensive?

The moment you observed her, you could no longer be sure . . . her gray eyes flashed with an unbearably hard brilliance. During the trial, if looks could have killed, she would most certainly have made mincemeat of the judge, the prosecutor, and the witnesses for the prosecution. Whenever she spoke, her words were caustic, peremptory; she had called some people imbeciles, or cretins, or narcissists, then gone on to tear their testimonies apart, and she was all the more formidable in that she had not missed the mark. It became difficult, after that, to rehabilitate those she had destroyed; nothing would grow again in the earth she had scorched. The sheer intelligence of this woman who didn't even seem to be intelligent made her diabolical. No matter what attitude she adopted, she was disturbing. Guilty? Her strict face was not vicious enough. Innocent? Her face lacked tenderness. So she had sold her body to graybeards? No, her body would have had to be desirable, desired, or at least desiring. Did she sincerely love those decrepit husbands of hers? No one could see any love in her at all.

The old woman took the two packages the butcher handed to her.

"Thank you, Marius."

The butcher shuddered. Behind the cash register his wife swallowed a hiccup. Coming from Marie Maurestier, the use of his first name was compromising. Apart from family and friends, no one in the village called Monsieur Isidore by his first name, because he wasn't the type to allow such familiarity. He was taken aback, and absorbed the shock, while his wife, teeth clenched, handed the change to Marie, not daring to say anything: she and her husband would sort things out later.

Marie Maurestier went out, wishing everyone a good day. Hasty, confused murmurs returned the courtesy.

In the street she ran into Yvette and her baby. Without greeting the mother, she went straight up to the infant.

"Hello my darling, what's your name?" she asked in a sugary voice.

At the age of four months, the child obviously could not reply, so Yvette answered for him.

"Marcello."

Still snubbing the mother, Marie smiled at the infant as if he were the one who had spoken.

"Marcello? What a pretty name . . . so much more elegant than Marcel."

"I think so too," said Yvette approvingly, satisfied.

"How many brothers and sisters do you have?"

"Two sisters, three brothers."

"So you're the sixth? Well that's very good, it's a good number."

"Oh, is it?" exclaimed Yvette, surprised.

Without answering her question, Marie continued her conversation with the child: "And why Marcello? Is your daddy Italian?"

The mother blushed. Everyone in the village knew that Yvette slept around and probably didn't know the identity of this father any more than any of the previous ones.

Turning at last to Yvette, Marie gave her a big smile and went into La Galette Dorée. The people in the boulangerie had been listening to her conversation with Yvette, and now they felt embarrassed.

Could one qualify Marie Maurestier's behavior just now as kind or malicious? It was impossible to say. When Marie Maurestier expressed an opinion, no one thought she was being sincere: she was pretending. Regardless of what she might be trying to convey through her gestures or her words, what came across, first and foremost, was control: by mastering the slightest flicker of her eyelashes, or modulating her voice with virtuosity, she seemed to be manufacturing compassion, anger, sobs, silences, or agitation. She was a fascinating actress because you could see her acting. With Marie, it was not that artifice was hidden to give an illusion of something natural; on the contrary, artifice confirmed the insincerity of her nature. Marie Maurestier was theatrical and never let herself go; she always preserved her self-awareness. Some people viewed this as proof of her falseness; others saw it as an expression of dignity.

"Half a baguette, please!"

No one bought half baguettes anymore except for Marie Maurestier; if anyone dared to try, the young baker became indignant and sent the miser packing. But the day he tried to explain to Marie that he sold an entire baguette or nothing at all, she replied, "Fine. The day you manage to bake a loaf of bread that does not go stale in three hours, I will buy one every other day. Let me know. Until then, I will buy half a baguette."

While she was waiting for her change, a tourist could not help but cry out, "Madame, would you be so kind as to give me your autograph in my notebook?"

Marie scowled, as if she might lose her temper, but then she said very clearly, "Of course."

"Oh thank you, Madame, thank you! I admire you so much, you know. I've seen all your programs on the television."

Marie gave the woman a look that meant "useless imbecile," appended her signature, handed back the notebook and left the boulangerie.

How did Marie Maurestier manage to live with fame that did not dwindle with time? While she may have given the ostensible impression that she bore it as a burden, certain details suggested that she also found it rather amusing; as a notable citizen, she found it perfectly natural to occupy a place of honor at festivals, weddings, and banquets. When the media wanted to question her or take her photograph, she immediately contacted her lawyer to negotiate a fee. The previous winter when she was bedridden with a nasty flu, she was secretly pleased when the inhabitants, concerned they might lose their historical monument, paraded past her house to ask for news. That summer, one roasting afternoon when she stopped off at the café to drink a peppermint cordial, she found herself short on cash and rather than apologize to the café owner, she merely said "With all the money I have brought you, the least you can offer me in return is a drink."

Slow, somewhat bent, as if her body were cumbersome, she went back the way she had come and began to climb the hill to her house. Over time she had become increasingly skilled at acting the victim; she was now remarkably good at maintaining her pose as victim of a judicial error. To be sure, in the beginning she committed a few blunders: for example, not long after her release, a mainstream magazine had pictured her in her garden—smiling, joyous, and carefree, stroking her cat or tending to her beloved roses. The effect was disastrous: such shocking cheerfulness did not befit either a widow—which was what she was—or a woman who has been broken by years of unjustified prison—which was what she was supposed to be; and as soon as the feature appeared, there came a slew of hateful articles in response, raising doubts, exploring the gray zones, trying to revive the hypothesis of her guilt. Subsequently therefore she had adopted a more humble profile, as if she were some great injured bird, and she did not deviate from it.

She walked up the street that ran through the heart of the village. On the hill, above the roofs and the bald plane trees, the vineyards extended in dull regularity, naked and dreary like a crop of barriers, in a month of March where only the gnarled vine stock wound its way around the wire supports.

As she went past the chapel she shuddered.

She could hear a hymn coming from the building. What? Could it be that . . .

Marie rushed up the steps as quickly as her arthritis and corns would allow, shoved open the door, which gave a resounding creak, and then, transfixed by the scene, she let the swirls of music enfold her like a heady perfume, brushing against her, caressing her, penetrating her.

A young priest was playing the harmonium.

His beauty was pure, indecent. He was alone in the nave, and radiant. His skin was as pale as if he were wearing powder, his lips drawn in the shape of a kiss, his form framed by a golden light that glided in perfect sympathy from the stained-glass window to his shoulders. Brighter than any altar, more appealing than the Christ on the cross, the source of subtle sounds that rose scrolling to the vaulted ceiling, the young priest had become the center of the church.

Marie was fascinated by his white hands as they caressed the keys, and she gazed at him with the emotion one feels in the presence of an apparition, until there came from outside the sound of a moped backfiring, which distracted their attention toward the entrance.

When he realized he had a visitor, the priest stopped playing and got up to greet her.

Marie Maurestier felt weak at the knees. He was thin, incredibly tall, in the way of a young yet manly adolescent, and he seemed to glow as he looked at her, like a lover meeting his mistress. As if he were on the verge of spreading his arms to welcome her.

"Greetings, my child. I am so pleased to have taken up this post in Saint-Sorlin. I have just left the monastery, and this is my first parish. I'm very fortunate, am I not, to have landed in such a pretty village?"

Disturbed by the deep, rich, velvety tones of his voice, Marie stammered that it was the village that should be pleased.

Briskly, he stepped closer.

"I am Abbé Gabriel."

She shuddered. An angelic name, in sharp contrast to the deep timbre of his voice.

"And to whom do I have the honor?" he asked, astonished that she had not introduced herself.

"Marie . . . "

She hesitated to reveal her name. She was afraid that her name, which had been splashed across so many pages of crime reports, might cast a pall, might spoil his childlike smile. Nevertheless, she took the chance.

"Marie Maurestier."

"I am delighted to meet you, Marie Maurestier."

Breathless, she noted that he had not recoiled—nor looked frightened or disapproving—when she revealed her identity: how extraordinary! So very unusual . . . He accepted her as she was, without judging, without locking her in a cage like some strange beast.

"Do you go to church sometimes, Marie?"

"I come to the service every day."

"You have never known a crisis of faith?"

"God would not tolerate my whims. If I did not live up to his expectations, he would quickly bring me up to his level."

She had wanted to share a humble thought and now she realized she had uttered a phrase filled with pride. To be up to God's level! That He would take the time to bring her up! The priest, after a moment's hesitation, was able to grasp the actual intention of her words.

"Faith is a grace," he said.

"Exactly! When our belief falters, God gives us a good kick in the ass to make us believe again."

She was astonished by her own words. "Kick in the ass!" Why had she used this expression that was utterly alien to her vocabulary? What had come over her? She was bawling like a drill sergeant, forthright, impetuous. Did she need to play at being a man when she was in the company of such a gentle soul? Confused, she lowered her eyes, ready to concede her mistake.

"Well, my child, shall we meet again at seven o'clock for the service?"

She rounded her lips to speak, then nodded. He's forgiven me, she thought. What a marvelous man!

The next morning she was the first to arrive at the church for the chilly morning mass.

When Abbé Gabriel came out of the sacristy, a green silk scarf over his immaculate alb, for a moment she was dazzled: he was just as fresh and charming as she remembered. Together they pushed the prie-dieu, set aside the chairs that were wobbly, arranged the bouquets, and piled up the prayer books, as if they were preparing a reception for their friends.

The village faithful arrived. Their average age was eighty,

their clothes were black and their hair was gray; they stood in small groups by the entrance, hesitating to come forward, not out of a sense of hostility toward the new priest but simply to express, through their reserve, how much they had appreciated his predecessor.

As if he understood, Abbé Gabriel went up to them, introduced himself, found the appropriate words to honor the former priest, who had died at the age of a hundred, then encouraged them to sit in the rows next to the choir.

As the priest walked up to the altar, Vera Vernet, who for Marie could be none other than "that old bag," murmured under her mustache, "They can't be serious, the bishop is making fun of us: he's much too young. They've sent us a seminarian!"

Marie smiled and did not answer. She felt as if she were attending a service for the first time. Through his fervor, through his commitment in every word and every gesture, Abbé Gabriel was reinventing the Christian mass. He quivered as he read the Gospel, and immersed himself in the prayers, eyes closed, as if his salvation depended upon it. The way he conducted the ritual spoke not of routine, but urgency.

Marie Maurestier looked at the venerable parishioners around her, and they seemed to have had their breath taken away by what was happening: it was as if they sat not in church pews but in the seats of an airplane breaking the sound barrier. Nevertheless, they allowed themselves to be swayed by the priest's ardor and gradually made it a point of honor not to behave like lukewarm Catholics. They stood, sat down, knelt, with good grace, whatever the hardship on their creaky joints; their singing was full throated; they recited the Lord's Prayer, making the words ring out, investing the formulas with meaning. After half an hour no one knew who was charming whom—the priest his flock or the flock their priest—their eagerness to outdo each other's enthusiasm was so great; even that goat Vera Vernet wore an inspired expression on her face when she went to take communion.

"Until tomorrow, Father," murmured Marie as she went down the chapel steps.

She shivered. How delightful, to say "Father" to a man who was so young, while she herself was so old!

As she left the service Marie had a radiant smile on her face, which she took home to hide. She was overjoyed that this priest had come, and it made her ridiculously proud: Gabriel's victory seemed to be hers, as well.

It did not take long for Gabriel to win over the village. In a few days his presence in the streets, at the café, and at the vicarage, where he started giving literacy classes in addition to the catechism, confirmed his favorable first impressions: people liked him, he was convincing. Before long the faithful from other villages were coming to attend mass. Saint-Sorlin was proud of having such a priest. Even the non-believers found him delightful.

Marie listened to the growing murmurs of approval as if she were receiving compliments about her own son. "My, they've certainly taken their time to realize what I knew right from the start."

Without realizing it, her exchanges with the priest were changing her. To be sure, her schedule and habits did not change, but now she experienced unexpected emotions as well.

At six o'clock sharp, the moment she got out of bed, she thought about how Gabriel was getting up at that time, too. While she was washing at her sink, naked in front of the mirror, she imagined him getting ready, naked as well, and how they would meet again soon. When she crossed the threshold of the church, breathless, she felt as if she were entering not just God's house, but Gabriel's, too. In the days of the old priest the church of Saint-Sorlin smelled of God the way a butcher's shop smells of dead meat, with faint, disgusting whiffs of decomposition; but ever since Gabriel had come, there were only scents of lily, incense, and beeswax; the stained-glass windows were clean, the tiles scrubbed, the tablecloths on the altar had been ironed: in short, it was as if God and the nice young man had set up housekeeping together in a cozy little bungalow.

The moment Gabriel, sparkling in his green silk scarf, opened the door to the sacristy and said, "Good morning, my children, I am delighted to see you," she took the words for herself. She complied with his orders: "Let us kneel," "Let us stand," "And now we shall sing," "Let us pray," in obedience to the man as much as to the liturgy. With great piety she drank in his every word. How very different her behavior was now from in the old days, when during the sermon she used to memorize the names and dates listed on the marble plaques along the aisle that were devoted to the great figures who had lived and died here! Thanks to Gabriel, the force and subtlety of the Gospels had been revealed to her, for not only did he tell them in a singular way, she could also see him in the role of Jesus—handsome, fragile, consumed by his love for humankind. She often imagined herself in the role of Mary Magdalene, and when she looked at Jesus-Gabriel she quivered with tenderness, nurturing him, then washing his feet and letting down her hair to dry them; the sacred stories took on meaning because they had become flesh.

What she found more difficult to bear was the sight of so many people showing up at church on Sundays, people who ordinarily never attended. One morning when she was alone with Gabriel she was compelled to criticize them.

"You know, Father, the Dubreuils, Morins, Desprairies and Isidores never used to come to mass before."

"So much the better, it's never too late. Remember the parable of the eleventh-hour workers."

"I wonder whether Jesus took into consideration what the

others might think, those who came early, only to see the late-comers so generously rewarded."

"He did think about it: he knew that those believers who had come early had all the time to nurture their own goodness."

Failing to grasp that his reply was aimed at her, enjoining her to show more kindness, she concluded huffily, "Yes, well . . . These sightseers have been coming to mass because it's something new for them. 'A new broom sweeps clean,' as my grandmother used to say."

"If they are coming out of curiosity, then it is up to me to keep them coming, my child. I hope I shall succeed."

She observed him—passionate, good, not an ounce of pettiness. She blushed, and was sorry she had been so negative. So it was in all sincerity that she proclaimed, "You will succeed, Father. You will make believers of them, of that I am sure."

In fact, what she really wanted was to obtain preferential treatment; she could put up with the priest taking care of everyone, provoking conversions, even miracles, so long as he continued to reserve a special regard for her. It would never have occurred to her to qualify her complicated feelings with the simple word jealousy.

Thus, she took a very dim view when Yvette suddenly burst into the chapel.

Yvette was a pair of thighs. While there are women who are noticed first and foremost for their eyes, mouth, or face, with Yvette it was her thighs. No matter how hard you tried to concentrate on her features when she was talking, the moment you could decently look away, you would stare at her thighs. Two warm, milky columns of flesh, the grain of her skin so fine that you would have liked to touch them, to ascertain their softness with your hand. No matter what Yvette was wearing, her thighs came first; when she wore a short dress you got the impression it had been cut in order to reveal her thighs, and her skirt would blow to one side so that her thighs could live;

shorts were mere sleeves for her thighs, and even trousers became molds for her thighs. Marie was so convinced that Yvette was nothing more than a pair of thighs that when Yvette spoke to her she did not even respond to the woman who was grafted upon them.

Still more pertinent was the fact that Yvette was the village whore. An occasional whore. When she didn't manage to make ends meet—which was every month—Yvette, with six mouths to feed, sold her body. And that was the whole problem: everyone considered her a whore, and accepted the fact—because you have to have one, as Marie's grandmother would have said—except Yvette herself. Consequently, the moment she overheard snide remarks or was met with a concupiscent gaze, she was hurt. She would act indignant, and cloak herself in her wounded pride, wearing the latest outrage she'd suffered on her lapel like a martyr's medal.

Marie thought she was ridiculous, but grew alarmed when she saw the obscene pair of thighs lurking around the priest.

"Filthy sow!"

Marie could not stand to see the young priest greeting Yvette attentively, or shaking her hand, or smiling at her the way he smiled at everyone.

"The poor man is so innocent that he doesn't even notice her little game. And yet he is still a man. She'll get there eventually . . . "

For Marie there could be no doubt: Yvette wanted to get the priest in the sack.

One afternoon when she came to change the flowers on the altar she saw Yvette burst out of the confession box, her thighs exposed, her eyelids swollen with tears, her face crimson with the flush of pleasure, and Marie thought the worst had occurred. It was all she could do not to run over and slap her. Fortunately Abbé Gabriel emerged in turn, looking peaceful, fresh, and pure. Marie let the young woman, visibly upset, leave the church with a slam of the door, then she went over to the vase with its withered bouquet.

The priest has just rejected her, thought Marie, and that's why the pair of thighs is furious.

Her heartbeat returned to normal as she replaced the rotting lilies with some she had just cut from her garden.

The priest came up to her, looking sad. She stared hard at him. He did not like being caught red-handed in a state of anxiety, and he turned away.

Marie decided to take advantage of this moment alone with him: "Yvette is pretty, isn't she?"

Astonished, he mumbled something. Marie insisted, "No? You don't think she's pretty?"

"I don't look at my flock in that way."

His voice was firmer. His sincerity reassured Marie, although her bad mood stayed with her, like a soup that continues to boil even after the flame beneath the pot has been put out.

"Father, I suppose you do know who Yvette is?"

"What do you mean?"

"She's the local prostitute. She didn't hide it from you, I hope?"

"She hid nothing from me: she is a great sinner. Why do you think I am devoting so much time to her?"

"You take a passionate interest in her sin?"

"Not at all. Am I not here to heal souls in distress? It's a paradox, in the end: I must devote more time to the dark souls than to the transparent ones."

His phrase was a moment of illumination. So was this the explanation? Abbé Gabriel devoted more care to vice than to virtue? Why had she not thought of this earlier?

"Father, would you hear my confession?"

They went into the waxed wooden box. Only a very thin latticework partition separated Marie from the young priest; it was as if she were touching him.

"Do you know, Father, that some years ago I was accused of having murdered several men?"

"Yes, I know, my child."

"They claimed that I poisoned my three husbands and bumped off a fourth man who was supposed to have been my lover!"

"Yes, I have heard tell of your ordeal. I also know that human justice has cleansed you."

"And so you will understand why I have very little respect for human justice."

"I don't understand . . . "

"I fear only God's justice."

"And so you should."

"For while I may be free of sin before man, before God I remain a grave sinner."

"Naturally. As do we all."

"Yes, but not to such a degree . . . "

She leaned closer and whispered, "I killed them."

"Who?"

"My three husbands."

"Oh, my God!"

"And my lover Rudy, too."

"Wretched woman!"

She added, with gleeful malice, "And his mistress, too, Olga, a Russian woman. And, just think, they never accused me because they never even noticed she had disappeared. Not a soul missed that cockroach."

"Jesus, Mary and Joseph, come to our aid as quickly as you can!"

The young priest crossed himself more in superstitious entreaty than out of elevated spirituality: the revelation of her crimes threw him into a panic.

Marie Maurestier relished his fright. And Yvette had been consigned to oblivion! Henceforth Marie would come first!

That day, she told him about the first of her murders. Not to shock him too greatly, or disgust him, she portrayed the poisoning as an act of compassion: her poor husband had been suffering so greatly that she acted more as a nurse than a homicide. To hear her speak, she hadn't murdered him so much as euthanized him, her Raoul.

The young priest listened, pale, reproachful, horrified.

He left without a word, merely making the sign of the cross over her.

The next morning, at the seven o'clock service, she could tell from the purple shadows under his eyes that he had slept poorly, or hardly at all.

After lunch, when he came to the confession box, he confirmed that he hadn't had enough sleep.

She was delighted by his admission: he was in her grip, he had tossed and turned in his bed, thinking about her. Since she had done the same, you might even say they had spent the night together.

That afternoon she again returned to her inaugural crime, Raoul, and instinctively, without really knowing why, she poured out the whole story in an entirely different way: darker, more realistic, accentuating her disgust for the old and senile Raoul, all her hatred for the way he forced her to touch him. Portraying herself as a young woman who was the victim of a libidinous fossil, she revealed her darkest feelings, her calculations, her criminal urges; she described in detail how she had poisoned him with arsenic over a period of nine months so that the dose would be fatal yet untraceable; her relief when he died, her role as the tearful widow at the funeral, her delight at receiving the money and the house without having to account to anyone ever again.

Every day she came to the church to unveil her crimes. Every night, the young man, obsessed by the tale of horrors, lost a few hours' sleep.

As she told her story, Marie reveled in being able to express herself at last, to free her memories and above all discover all her unsuspected motives. For while there was no changing the fact of the murders, her reasons for committing them varied from one day to the next. Which was the actual reason? The one on Tuesday, or Wednesday, or Friday, or Saturday? All of them. She relished every nuance; for years she had always had to stick to the "not guilty" version, so now exploring the "guilty" version enabled her to grasp the complexity of her behavior, the infinite varieties of her intentions; Marie was jubilant over the rich, diverse, profound character of her inner self . . . And she had been granted an additional faculty: while she may have had the power of life or death over a man in the past, she now exerted control over the truth of her acts, as she scrounged and interpreted and reexamined, destroying clichés and becoming the author of her own story.

She established her ascendancy over the young priest. He no longer slept. Incapable of taking an interest in anything else, he anticipated as much as he dreaded their meetings at the confession box. His freshness faded. It was as if Marie were taking him away, into her world, her age, her fatigue, her ugliness . . . Naturally she did not realize this, and continued to see him just as she always had.

The most intense moment for the priest and the sinner was when she spoke of her lover, Rudy the surfer, who had given her the only sensual pleasure of her entire life, a pleasure that was all the more vigorous for its total unexpectedness, for Marie had not enjoyed sex at all until Rudy. Surprised to find herself thinking about a man from morning to night, she had initially believed that she loved him for love's sake until she realized it was above all his caresses that she wanted, his body against hers, the blond duvet on his skin, the smell of him. There was something about Rudy that annoyed her, attracted her, titillated her; he knew how to create a sensual atmosphere around him, which was powerful in his presence, then exasperating the moment he left. As she told Gabriel about this man she had desired to distraction, she was overcome by a confused, torrid feverishness, where the past contaminated the present; she left the confession box consumed by an urge to kiss the young man's lips, to tear off his cassock and explore the texture of his skin with her fingers. Her passion for Gabriel intensified by a notch.

In the rising warmth of springtime, their daily tête-à-tête in the cramped confession box became suffocating. By the time they parted, they were both exhausted, drained, but they had regained their strength by the time of their next meeting.

She took a bawdy pleasure in shocking Gabriel, almost as if they were in bed together and she was finding ways to make him relax by sharing episodes of sensual refinement—bold, unexpected, taboo. For example, she insisted upon the brutality with which she had drowned her lover: it had been pure impulse. It is true that Rudy had drunk so much that night that he no longer had the vigor nor the necessary wisdom to resist her in the bathtub. She then emphasized the sangfroid with which she concealed her crime; she loved to tell of how she and her sister Blanche rolled the corpse up in a carpet, dumped it in the back of a stolen car, drove seven hundred kilometers, boarded a boat in Brittany in the pitch of night, tossed the corpse with its weight of stones into the dark water, returned in the early hours of the day, scrubbed the car inside out, and finally abandoned it with all its keys in the middle of a parking lot known to be the hangout of gangs who, they hoped, would leave their prints all over it. This all happened far from Saint-Sorlin, in Biarritz, where she had rented a house with the inheritance from her three husbands.

For the first time in her life she revealed the episode with Olga, Rudy's mistress, the one he saw regularly between his liaisons with women of a certain age. Olga had begun to fret over the absence of her man, and she burst into Marie's house screaming that she suspected her of bumping him off and that she would denounce her to the police. Betraying neither emotion nor fear, Marie had assured her that Rudy had gone abroad and had entrusted Marie with a sum of money to give to Olga. With the lure of gain, the lie became credible: the Russian woman now thought better of going to the police. Marie arranged to meet her that night on the terrace of a bar popular with all the local young people. There she handed her an envelope containing a few bank notes, and promised her the rest of the money the next day; she slipped poison into the young woman's cocktail and left her in the company of the revelers.

Although neither the press nor the authorities ever mentioned Olga's disappearance, Marie was convinced that the young woman had died, because she had never come to claim the rest of the money she was owed.

All this talk about murder, the underworld, blackmail, and corruption made Gabriel feel faint. Marie could sense his distress; it was as if she were initiating him to real life, to the world the way it truly is, hostile and violent. In a way, she was teaching him a thing or two.

And henceforth Yvette could go and cry all alone in a corner, for now Gabriel pushed her away, assuring her that he would spend time with her as soon as he had the opportunity. He sent the other penitents packing as well. While he still said mass, and magnificently, he was no longer free: he was obsessed by the poisoner's confessions, haunted by her murders. Marie Maurestier had won. She reigned over Abbé Gabriel, and over the village.

Marie was enchanted that he was now the guardian of her secrets, and she thrilled to see how he lied about her, standing up to those bitter old hags who came to quack in their ugly duck-like voices that they were surprised he devoted so much time to her.

"You're not going to tell us she's innocent, now are you, Father? Otherwise why would she spend so much time in the confession box?"

"Her soul has suffered great injustice—like the horrible accusations you yourself are bringing against her at this very moment, my child, without even a trace of kindness."

He was better than a confidante; he was an accomplice. They shared not only the truth but also the crime. Were they not committing a crime together?

Their complicity intoxicated her.

After five weeks of confession she realized she had told her story until there was nothing left to tell. She came up with a few more misdeeds she had committed during her two trials, but she knew that she was emptying her last rounds and soon she would have no more ammunition.

She was afraid the bell might be tolling for her supremacy.

That Wednesday, the young priest informed his flock that he would be absent the following day and the day after. Just like that! With no further information, and out of the blue! Nor did he divulge anything to Marie.

What was going on?

Was he avoiding her because she no longer fed his shocked curiosity? She wasn't about to go inventing new crimes, now was she! Was she supposed to lie in order to keep him, or turn herself into Scheherazade?

The long hours without Gabriel seemed unbearable. She was in pain. Here she had bared her soul to the priest: was this all she would get, his silence, his sudden absence? In the end, Gabriel was no better than the others.

Weary, disgusted, depressed, on Friday evening at seven o'clock she discovered a rash on her ankles. To punish herself for waiting for him, she placed her feet on a stool and scratched her ankles until they bled. The house was creaking with boredom. In the scent of oilcloth that filled her dwelling, she could not focus her attention on anything, neither the rusty horseshoe on the windowsill, nor the postman's calendar, let alone the newspapers full of classified ads.

At eight o'clock, someone rang at her door.

It was Gabriel.

She was overjoyed. He may have gone away, but she was the first person he had come to upon his return. She hid her legs, asked him to come in, offered him something to eat or drink. He declined, with a grave expression, and insisted on standing.

"Marie, I have thought a great deal about what you have told me, these terrible revelations of which I am now the mute guardian—a silent guardian, because I shall never betray the secret of the confession. You see, I went away for two days to think. I conferred with my bishop, and with the priest who trained me at the seminary. Without mentioning your name, I described your case to them in order to know how I should behave. I've come to a decision. A decision that concerns us both."

As solemnly as if he were asking her hand in marriage, he seized her wrists, firmly. She shuddered.

"You have revealed your sins to God."

He squeezed her fingers.

"Now you must confess your sins to mankind."

Marie withdrew her hands and stepped back.

He insisted.

"Yes, Marie! You must take responsibility for your crimes. It's better for justice. Better for the families of the victims. Better for the truth."

"I don't give a damn about the truth!"

"No. The truth is important to you because you have told me the truth."

"I told you! Only you! No one else!"

Horrified, she realized that he hadn't understood her at all. She had not been serving the truth, she had been using the truth! She had only used it so that she could captivate him, charm him. It was not as he thought, she had not been speaking to God but to him and him alone.

He shook his head.

"I want you to free yourself in the eyes of man, too. Go back to see the judge and tell him everything."

"Confess? Never! I didn't fight all those years for that! I can see that you're not the one who had to go through two trials . . . I won, do you understand? I won!"

"What did you win, Marie?"

"My honor, my reputation."

"A false honor . . . a false reputation . . . "

"Where honor and reputation are concerned, it's only appearances that matter."

"And yet you did sacrifice your honor and your reputation. You came to me with your burden."

"To you, yes. To you alone."

"To God, too."

"Yes . . . "

"But God, like me, has accepted you just as you are: guilty. And God, like me, continues to love you."

"Oh, really?"

He took her hands again, kneading them in his own, so warm and soft.

"Tell the truth, Marie, tell it to everyone. I will help you, I will support you. That will be my goal from now on. I am living in this village for that purpose alone, for your sake; you are the purpose of my life, you are the reason I pray, the reason I believe. Marie, you are my mission. I will change everything in you, I will bring to life the true Christian who is in you. With the fire of my faith, I will light your own. Together we will succeed. You will do it for me, and for yourself, and for God."

Marie gazed at him with new eyes. His mission? Had she heard him properly? She was his mission?

When she smiled, he thought he was going to win.

The summer months that followed were the happiest she had ever known. Gabriel no longer left her. He got up to see her, he opened the church so that she could come in, he ate his meals quickly so that he could be with her all the sooner, he heard her confession every afternoon and then, in the vicarage, in his house, or in her living room, he spoke to her endlessly—inspired, ablaze, passionate.

Marie took cynical pleasure in her privilege: she had wrenched Gabriel away from the others. She'd won! She had won yet again! He could talk and smile all he liked, and make his gentle gestures and his subtle arguments, she would not obey him. It was pointless, because he was the one who was obeying her.

Yet in her happiness she did not take into account the power of conviction that inhabited the priest.

There was a trap she had failed to see: by insisting, Gabriel was leading her onto the terrain of exchange and discussion. Already in July, not to be outdone, she answered him, grew bolder, ventured into the field of ideas. And this was a terrain where he was better prepared than she was. Progressively, without her actually realizing, while she imagined she was resisting him, he was influencing her, transforming her, suggesting new foundations for her ideas, and instilling ideals in her that until now had always been foreign.

She no longer spoke about God the way she used to.

God used to belong to her collection of weaponry; she would say "God" the way you fire a gun; peremptorily, with the way she said "God" in a loud voice she could obtain silence, she could chase intruders, and create a void around her. Sometimes, to reinforce her arguments, she would quote pell-mell from the Gospels and the Fathers of the Church, scattering shot against her adversaries to rebuff them or hurt them, if she couldn't kill them; she aimed quickly, precisely, fired right in the bull's eye. God had enabled her in succession to establish her virtuous reputation and endure the petty quarrels that others picked with her.

Now she saw God not as a terrible, avenging god but as a fount of tenderness. When Gabriel, who said "our dear Lord" rather than "God," murmured the name of the Creator, he gave the impression he was evoking a vital source, the best wine to drink, or even a remedy for every ill. By his side, Marie was initiated into a new theology; she renounced her former sheriff for the god of love, a kindly, merciful Jesus, six foot four inches in height, like Gabriel, and who had Gabriel's features.

Before Gabriel came into her life, she had forced herself to observe a narrow, repetitive piety, reassuring in its very boredom. But now she was passionately interested in the essence of the prayers and sermons; she even read the Gospels from time to time in the evening.

In fact, she did not realize that he was gaining powerful influence over her. While the origins of that influence may have been sexual, the reality had become spiritual. Marie dreamed of Good, she was moved by stories of forgiveness, she attained ecstasy when he told her stories of the saints, particularly Saint Rita, whom he had studied and made the subject of his dissertation at the seminary.

"Patron saint of lost causes? Then she is my patron saint," thought Marie as she went to bed.

They spent long hours together locked in battle, which drained him and filled her with enthusiasm.

She believed that she was in control of the situation as always, when in fact it was Gabriel who was expanding his dominion. She shivered in his presence.

"Overwhelm me,'" she seemed to be saying with each sentence. "Do with me what you like."

This was the first time she had ever encountered the bliss of submission. For while the young man may not have penetrated her physically, he dominated her intellectually; by letting herself be manipulated, she experienced the fulfillment of the masochist who allows herself to grow attached. The violence in her soul was finding an outlet. All her life this tormented creature had played at being the strong, hard woman, and now at last she was discovering her true nature: a slave. By leaving her own self behind she found repose. The drive to control had given way to abandonment; she succumbed to a sensual, dizzying delight as she became an object in Gabriel's hands and mind.

One day, irritated because she had tried his patience, he exclaimed, red with anger, pointing his finger at her: "You are the devil, but I will turn you into an angel."

That day she shivered to the depths of her body, from her thighs to her scalp, a sort of orgasm that occurred nightly whenever she recalled the scene.

From that moment on she lowered her guard. She thought like him, felt like him, breathed like him.

"You and I are possessed by Good," he declared.

She thought: With you, I will follow Good and Evil equally, since I am in your possession. But she did not argue with him.

But still she resisted and did not relent altogether. In the evening, alone, she went into raptures, telling herself again and again that yes, she would confess her crimes to mankind, yes, she would sacrifice her comfort for the sake of righteousness. And yet every morning her courage failed her.

"If I agree, will you come to see me in prison?"

"Every day, Marie, every day. If I manage to convince you, we will be bound forever. Not only before mankind but also before God."

A marriage, in a way . . . Yes, surely, he was asking her to marry him.

More and more often, she imagined herself describing their union *urbi et orbi*, to the television, to journalists, to the police, to the judges. "He's the one, Abbé Gabriel, who persuaded me to reveal everything. Without him I would have continued to deny my crimes. Without him, I would have taken the truth with me to my grave. Gabriel has not only made me believe in God, he has made me believe in man." In her daydreams, this woman, never a talkative sort, became downright eloquent, and she could wax on forever about the metamorphosis she owed to the young man. She hoped they would take a picture of the two of them, either in court or in the visitors' room at the prison.

To be sure, there were moments when she realized that their situation would not be equal: he would be free, she'd be in prison. But is one free when one is a priest? No. Does one despair when, every day, one receives the visit of the person one loves? Not to any greater degree. Does love not require one to favor the other?

"Sacrifice is the measure of all love."

That is what Gabriel had said in one of his sermons from the pulpit. Marie had immediately understood that he was addressing her, and she was resolved to apply the maxim: she would sacrifice herself! So that the entire world would know that Gabriel was a great priest, she would confess. So that the entire world would learn of the power this young man had over her, she would embrace her punishment. So that the entire world would remember them as an extraordinary couple, she would embrace her penance. She could not give a child to Gabriel, so she would replace that child with glory: she would make him a media success, give him a judicial scandal and a place in History; their twin performance would be the subject of conversation for many years—how she had deceived justice so extravagantly during her trials, how he had left his spiritual imprint upon a terrible sinner. Without him Marie would have remained irredeemable. A lost cause. Thank you, Saint Rita, for inspiring him. When the history of morality meets the history of saints . . . No more, no less. And anyway, who knows? Perhaps for Gabriel it could even lead to Rome?

In a state of exaltation, she yielded to a multitude of feverish dreams.

After that incredible summer, with its wealth of torment and emotion, she arose one day on the cusp of autumn and felt changed.

That Sunday she went to mass, silent and concentrated. After the service she went home and found she could not swallow a thing. Her cat relished the steak she had bought for herself.

At two o'clock she went to the vicarage and informed Gabriel that she would confess.

"I swear upon it, Father. On God and on you."

He took her in his arms and held her close. She tried to weep, in order to stay a bit longer against his tall warm body, but there was nothing for it, she managed only a shrill, ridiculous hiccup.

He congratulated her, told her dozens of times over that he was proud of her, of her faith, of the path she had come thus far, then he enjoined her to kneel beside him in order to thank the Lord.

While they were going through their phrases, Marie's head was spinning. Her decision had left her dizzy and she was overcome by emotion, the emotion of being so close to him, shoulder to shoulder in a moment of intimacy, and she was engulfed by the smell of his skin and hair. She thought of how from now on he would come every day to the prison to pray with her like this, and she would be happy.

After she left him, she climbed to the top of the village. At peace, she spent her last night of freedom looking out at Saint-Sorlin from the highest point in the vineyards: a sunset first mauve then violet cast its mournful colors over the fields. Cats scampered onto the tiled roofs to observe the passing of the day; against the dying sky, dozens of them formed a sacred company, a décor of silhouettes made holy as shadowgraphs.

She would go this week to Bourg-en-Bresse to find the judge who had opened the file for the investigation; he had been a young man at the time, and he despised her because her acquittal had robbed him of the promotion ensured by the condemnation of a woman who had poisoned her husbands. He would be eager to hear what she had to say.

Here and there a few lights glowed in the darkness, outlining a roof, a room, a street corner. Behind her a Labrador sat under a swing licking her puppies; the linden trees filled the garden with fragrance like a sickly sweet herbal tea. "Tomorrow, my fellow villagers, you will wake up in a village that has become even more famous, the village of Marie Maurestier, the demon who has become an angel, the murderess who had fooled everyone but would not fool God. She began as Messalina and she will end her life as a saint." Marie felt as if she were somehow contagious, as if she were doing good to others, bringing them the light, the light she had received from Gabriel. "Ladies and gentlemen, I met a prodigious priest. He was not a man, he was an angel. Without him I would not be here before you." She would be able to talk about him, about their intimate relationship, to the entire world. So many wonderful things to come . . .

She gazed at the stars, prayed to God to help her find courage and submission, or rather the courage of submission. She did not go home until it was pitch black.

As she was turning her key in the lock, her neighbor opened her shutters and called out, "The priest was looking for you. He came twice."

"Oh, did he? Thank you for telling me. I'll go to the vicarage."

"I don't think you'll find him there. A car came and took him away just now."

A car? Of course he did not drive, and he didn't even have a car.

Marie went to the vicarage. Behind the drawn curtains the interior was dark and empty. She knocked on the door, knocked again, pounded. In vain. There was no one.

She went back to her house, refusing to worry. It hardly mattered, she was firm in her resolution, and the priest was glad of it. No doubt he had wanted to compliment her one more time and offer to accompany her to Bourg-en-Bresse, who knows. She calmed down, certain there would be an explanation in the morning.

And indeed, her phone rang at dawn. The moment she recognized Gabriel's voice, she was immediately reassured.

"My dear Marie, the most extraordinary thing has happened."

"What is it, dear Lord?"

"I've been appointed to the Vatican."

"Pardon?"

"The Holy Father read my memoir about Saint Rita. He liked it so much that he has asked me to join a theological study group at the papal library."

"But . . . "

"Yes. It means I am obliged to leave you. Both you and Saint-Sorlin."

"But our project?"

"It changes nothing. You have made your decision."

"But . . . "

"You will go through with it, since you made your promise. To me and to God."

"But you won't be there by my side! When I go to prison you won't be coming to visit me every day."

"You will do as you said, because you promised me."

"You and God, I know . . . "

She hung up, disturbed, wavering between the ecstasy in which she had spent the previous day and anger. "The Vatican . . . He was supposed to be going to the Vatican because of me. The Holy Father was going to congratulate him on my confession. He could have waited just a little longer. It's still better to go to the Vatican because you've done the impossible, because you've obtained the redemption of a criminal, than because of yet another text about some minor saint. What is the matter with him? How could he betray me like this?"

Two days later Vera Vernet, the "old bag" with her body as twisted as a vine stock, came to inform Marie in her sharp voice that a new priest had arrived.

Marie went to the church.

In his tight gray cassock with worn seams, the priest was sweeping the steps outside the church, chatting with the inhabitants of Saint-Sorlin.

When she saw him—short, ruddy, with thick features, a man well into his fifties—Marie Maurestier immediately knew how she was going to spend the years to come: she would tend her garden, feed her cat, go less often to mass and remain silent until her dying day.

THE RETURN

"G reg . . ."

"I'm working."

"Greg . . ."

"Leave me alone, I've got twenty-three more pipes to clean."

Greg refused to turn around and leaned over the second turbine, his powerful back and prominent muscles stretching his cotton singlet fit to burst.

Dexter the sailor insisted: "Greg, the captain's waiting for you."

Greg whirled so suddenly that Dexter jumped. With sweat streaming from his naked shoulders to his lower back, the huge man was transformed into a barbarian idol: an aura of evaporation suffused his body as it gleamed with the wild flames of the boilers. Thanks to his talents as an engineer, seven days a week, twenty-four hours a day, the freighter *Grandville* sailed its course without flagging, crossing oceans to transport goods from one port to another.

"Have I done something wrong?" asked the burly fellow, creasing his brown eyebrows that were as thick as a finger.

"No. He's waiting for you."

Greg nodded, feeling guilty already. Convinced he was right he said again, "He's going to tell me I've done something wrong."

A shiver of pity chilled Dexter the messenger, for he knew why Greg was being called to the captain, and he didn't want to tell him.

"Don't be stupid, Greg. How could he find fault with you? You do more work than four men put together."

But Greg was no longer listening. Resigned, wiping the black grease off his hands with a rag, he accepted the fact he was going to be told off, because discipline on board was far more important to him than his own pride: if his superior had something to fault him with, he must have a good reason.

Greg didn't delve any further into the matter because he knew the captain would tell him soon enough. As a rule, Greg avoided thinking. He wasn't good at it and, above all, he figured he wasn't being paid to think. As far as the contract he had with his employer went, if he were to spend his time thinking it would seem like a betrayal to him, all that time wasted and energy lost. He was working as hard at the age of forty as he had worked in the beginning when he was fourteen: up at dawn, all over the ship until nightfall, cleaning, repairing, fiddling with the spare parts, he seemed to be obsessed by a need to do things well, as if he were tormented by an insatiable devotion that nothing could diminish. The only reason he went to relax on his narrow bunk with its thin mattress was so he could get back to work.

He put on a plaid shirt, threw on a foul-weather jacket, and followed Dexter up on deck.

The sea was in a bad temper today, neither raging nor calm, just in a bad temper. Foam splattered from short, ominous waves. As is often the case in the Pacific, the world seemed monochromatic, because the gray sky had imposed its concrete hue upon all the elements—the waves, clouds, floors, pipes, tarpaulins, and men; even Dexter, whose skin ordinarily shone copper, now wore the anthracite complexion of boiled cardboard.

Struggling against the howling wind, the two men reached the wheelhouse. Once they'd closed the door behind them, Greg felt intimidated: far from the roaring of the machines or of the ocean, torn from the pungent smells of fuel and algae, he no longer felt like he was on board ship, it was more like some drawing room on land. A few men, including the first mate and the radio operator, were standing stiffly around their captain.

"Sir," he said looking down, in a form of surrender.

Captain Monroe replied, mumbled a few words, then hesitantly cleared his throat.

Greg remained silent, waiting to be sentenced.

Greg's humility did not encourage Monroe to speak. He looked over at his subordinates as if to consult them; they had no desire to be in his shoes. When he felt he was going to lose his crew's respect if he delayed much longer, Captain Monroe, neglecting the emotional charge which accompanied the information he had to convey, kept his tone curt, his delivery staccato, as he said:

"We received a telegram message for you, Greg. A family problem."

Grey looked up, astonished.

"In fact, it's bad news," continued the captain. "Very bad news. Your daughter has died."

Greg's eyes opened wide. For the time being only surprise filled his face, and no other emotion was visible.

The captain insisted: "That's it. Your family doctor in Vancouver, Dr. Simbadour, contacted us. We don't know anything more. We are very sorry, Greg. My sincere condolences."

Greg's expression still had not changed: his features frozen with surprise, pure surprise, no emotion.

No one around him said a word.

Greg looked at each of them in turn as if they might have an answer to his question; as he did not find it, he eventually said, "My daughter? Which daughter?"

"I beg your pardon?" said the captain, startled.

"Which of my daughters? I have four."

Monroe blushed. Afraid he might have written the message

down wrong, he took it out of his pocket and with trembling hands read it once again.

"Hmm . . . no. There is nothing else. This is all it says: we regret to inform you that your daughter has died."

"Which one?" insisted Greg, more annoyed by the lack of precise details than fully cognizant of what they were telling him. Kate? Grace? Joan? Betty?

The Captain read the message over and over, hoping for a miracle, that between the lines he might suddenly find a name. Flat and succinct, the text was limited to those words alone.

At a loss, Monroe handed the paper to Greg, who deciphered it in turn.

The engineer nodded, sighed, turned the paper this way and that and then handed it back to the captain.

"Thank you."

The captain almost murmured, "You're welcome," then understood it was absurd, mumbled in his beard, fell silent, and stared out to port at the horizon.

"Is that all?" asked Greg, looking up, his eyes as clear as if nothing had happened.

The other sailors in the room were dumbfounded. They thought they had misheard. The captain, who had to reply, did not know how to react. Greg insisted, "Can I go back to work now?"

In the presence of such placid behavior the captain, who felt a sting of revulsion, endeavored to add some humanity to the absurd scene:

"Greg, we will not get to Vancouver for another three days. Would you like us to try in the meantime to contact the doctor for more information?"

"Could you?"

"Yes. We don't have his contact information since he called from company headquarters, but with a bit of good luck, we can get back to the source and—"

"Yes, that would be better."

"I'll take care of it in person."

"Right," said Greg, speaking like a robot, "it would be better, after all, if I knew which of my daughters . . . "

And there he had to pause. Just as he was about to say the word, he realized what had happened: one of his children had lost her life. He stopped with his mouth open, his face went crimson, his legs gave way. He clung with one hand to the chart table to keep from falling.

Around him the men were almost relieved to see him react at last. The captain came up and patted him on the shoulder.

"I'll take care of it, Greg. We'll get to the bottom of the mystery."

Greg glanced at the hand that was causing his damp slicker to squeak. The captain removed his hand. They stood there, embarrassed, neither one daring to look the other in the eye, Greg from a fear of expressing his pain, the captain from a fear of receiving his distress right in the face.

"Take the day off, if you want."

Greg stiffened. The prospect of not working filled him with anxiety. What would he do if he didn't work? The shock restored his speech.

"No, I'd rather not."

Every man in the room envisioned the torture Greg would endure in the hours ahead. A prisoner of the ship—mute and alone, he must be crushed by a sorrow as heavy as their cargo, tormented by a horrible question: which one of his daughters had died?

Back in the engine room, Greg went to work the way you rush into the shower when you're covered with mud; never before had the pipes been cleaned, scrubbed, polished, readjusted, or tightened with so much energy and care as that afternoon.

However, despite his labor, a thought occurred to him and wormed its way into his brain. Grace . . . His second daughter's face took over his imagination. Was it Grace who had died? Grace was fifteen, with an explosive love of life, her face radiant with smiles, energetic and carefree: was she not also the sickliest? Had her cheerfulness not given her a nervous strength which made her look healthy, but did not make her sturdier or more resistant for all that? Was she not the one who had brought home every single illness her schoolmates could pass on to her from the nursery, school, or high school? Grace was too good-natured, always ready for anything—games, friendships, viruses, bacteria, germs. Greg told himself he would no longer experience the happiness of seeing her walk and jump and tilt her head to one side and raise her arms and laugh out loud.

It was Grace. There could be no doubt.

Why was he thinking like this? Was it an intuition? Was he receiving some telepathic information? He stopped scrubbing for a moment. No, in fact, he didn't know; he was afraid. If he thought it was her, it was because Grace . . . was his favorite daughter.

He sat back, flabbergasted by his discovery. Never before had he established any type of hierarchy. So, he had a favorite . . . Had he shown it? To her or the others? No. His preference had been hidden deep inside: obscure, active, and inaccessible even to himself until now.

Grace . . . He thought tenderly about the young girl with her wild hair and long neck. It was so easy to like her. She was brilliant, less thoughtful than her elder sister, more lively than the others, unacquainted with boredom, and no matter the situation she could come up with a thousand details to make it entertaining. He could tell he would suffer if he went on thinking she was no more. So he went back to work with a vengeance.

"Provided it's not Grace!"

He tightened the bolts until the wrench slipped from his hands.

"It would be better if it was Joan."

To be sure, Joan's loss would be less of a blow. Joan was abrupt, angular, somewhat sullen, with shiny brown hair as thick as hay growing low on her forehead. A little rat-like face. He felt he had nothing in common with her. She was the third daughter, it had to be said, so she did not enjoy either the effect of novelty that their first child had brought, nor the sense of tranquility they felt by the time the second child arrived. The third one was taken for granted, they paid less attention to her, her sisters would look after her. Greg had not seen much of her because she was born while he was working for a new company that sailed all the way to the Emirates. And he really didn't like her coloring, either her skin or eyes or lips; he could see neither his wife nor his other daughters in her when he looked at her; she was like a stranger to him. Oh, he had no doubt she was his daughter, because he remembered the night they had conceived her—he had just gotten back from Oman—and the neighbors often said how much she looked like him. She had the same head of hair, that much was certain. Maybe that's why he felt ill at ease with her: a girl who had all the characteristics of a boy without being a boy.

For Greg had produced only daughters, his semen was incapable of generating any males, not strong enough to induce Mary's belly to bring forth anything but females. And he blamed himself for it. He was the one, the man, who was responsible for the masculine side of the couple, he was the giant who for some unknown and above all invisible reason was lacking the virility necessary to impose a boy on this mold for girls.

In all likelihood Joan had very nearly turned into a boy . . . She was a tomboy, and as such bore witness to Greg's deficiency. Moreover, he bristled whenever anyone complimented him on his gaggle of girls, because he sensed some insidious mockery at work.

"You are so lucky, Mr. Greg, to have four daughters! Girls adore their dad. They must idolize you, no?"

Of course they loved him. All the trouble he went to for their sake—never at home, always at sea working to provide money for the house, food, clothes, studies . . . of course they loved him! They would be a darn sight ungrateful if they didn't, his entire paycheck went straight to them, he only ever had crumbs left over for himself. Of course they loved him . . .

In Greg's opinion, love was a duty, or something you were owed. Since he sacrificed himself for his daughters, they owed him their affection. And he expressed his loyalty as a father by working like a dog. He could never have suspected that love might consist of smiles, caresses, tenderness, laughter, presence, games, time offered and time shared. He had every reason, in his own eyes, to consider himself a good father.

"Then it's Joan who died."

Although he couldn't come out and say it, this hypothesis eased his suffering.

In the evening, when the captain called him up to the bridge, Greg expected Monroe to confirm his suspicion.

As he stood before his superior, Greg was astonished to find himself thinking, in the form of a short, insistent prayer: *Above all, he mustn't say Grace's name. Not Grace, but Joan. Joan. Joan.*

"My poor fellow," exclaimed the captain, "we haven't been able to contact anyone at all. Because of the sky, the sea, connections are very poor. In short, we don't know which daughter . . . "

"Thank you, Sir."

Greg saluted and went out.

He ran to his cabin and locked himself in, his ears burning with shame. Had he not just wished for the death of one of his daughters? Had he not chosen the one they could take from him? What right had he to do that? Who had authorized him to whisper Joan's name to the captain? By designating her, was he not behaving like a murderer? Were the treacherous thoughts swirling in his brain worthy of a father? A loyal father would fight to save his daughters, all his daughters . . .

Disgusted with himself, he stamped his feet in his narrow cell; he struck the metal wall several times with his fist.

"Shame! Shame! If someone says 'your daughter,' you think of Grace. And if someone says, 'your daughter has died,' you throw Joan into the grave. You should die of shame."

To be sure, no one had heard him thinking, but he himself had: he now knew that he was vile and despicable. He would never recover from this bleeding wound.

"I don't have the right to love Joan less than the others. Nor do I have the right to love Grace more. Why haven't I been thinking of Kate or Betty?"

Just as he was ranting to himself, Dexter knocked on the door.

"Are you okay, Greg?"

"I'm okay."

"Don't you go saying just any old thing. Give me a minute. I've got something that will help you."

Greg yanked open the door and said, almost violently, "No one can help me."

Dexter nodded, but handed him a book all the same.

"Here."

"What's this?"

"My Bible."

Greg was so disconcerted that he forgot his sorrow for a few seconds. His hands refused to take the Bible, and his eyes, full of hostility, took in the old stained canvas cover, and everything inside him cried out, "What the fuck do you want me to do with this?"

"Keep it, just in case . . . Maybe you'll come upon a text that could help you."

"I don't read."

"Open the Bible; it's not reading, it's thinking."

Dexter shoved the volume into his hands and went off to prepare for his watch.

Greg tossed the book onto his mattress, realized that he wouldn't be able to get to sleep, put on his sneakers and his jacket and decided to jog on deck until he collapsed with fatigue.

The next morning Greg woke up convinced that Joan had died.

And this time, it no longer suited him, on the contrary, it hurt him: he dreamt that Joan was dying because she had a bad father, an indifferent parent. Still in bed he began to sob over his daughter's fate, her short life spent with a brutal man, for while he may have hidden from Grace the fact that he preferred her, he had made it quite clear to Joan that he had a hard time putting up with her—he was always scolding her, correcting her, asking her to be quiet or let her sisters speak. Had he ever really hugged her willingly? The child must have felt that he was reluctant to approach her, and if he did so it was more out of a concern for equal treatment than because he felt an impulse to hug her.

Tossing and turning in his bed he felt the weight of Dexter's Bible on his thigh. He began to leaf through the tome unconsciously, wearily gazing at the verses that were printed in such small type, skimming the table of contents, and among the pages he found a card. It was a holy picture, colorful and naïve, printed in relief on meringue-colored card stock, a golden halo framing a woman's face, that of Saint Rita.

He was moved by her smile. It symbolized his wife and daughters in their purity, beauty and candor.

"Please don't let it be Joan," murmured Greg to the picture, "please don't let it be Joan. That way I'll be able to make it up to her. I'll give her the attention and affection she deserves. Please don't let it be Joan."

He was surprised to find himself speaking to a cardboard figure; he would have been just as surprised if he'd found himself in the presence of the saint in flesh and blood, for he did not believe in God or in saints. But Dr. Simbadour's telegram had left him in such a state that he was ready to try anything, including prayer. However much he may have wanted Joan to disappear last night, today he wanted her to live so that he could make up for lost time and the rarity of tenderness he'd shown her.

He went back to work, less energetically, because now his ruminations were absorbing part of his strength. The news had stirred up a painful world of thoughts: the door of mental suffering had now opened to him.

He thought about his eldest daughter, Kate, the silent one, who was like her mother physically and like her father in character; at the age of eighteen she was already working in a store in Vancouver . . . Had she died at work? If it was Kate, what dreams had this death come to interrupt?

Greg realized that he didn't really know his daughters. He could list objective facts about them—their age, habits, schedules—but he was completely oblivious as to what troubled their minds. Familiar strangers. Enigmas who depended on his authority. Four daughters: four unknown quantities.

He examined himself in the mirror. He was sturdy, with square shoulders and square ideas. His physique did not lie: his narrow forehead, wider than it was high, left little room for intellect; broad thighs supporting an ample pelvis, although it was not as ample as his torso which grew wider as it rose, powerful, to his shoulders. His body told the story of a man who devoted himself to physical activity. Every evening for years he had been proud to wear himself out, because his exhaustion gave him a sense of duty fulfilled. A very simple life, not even subject to the wearing of time, because to grow tired of one thing one must imagine the next . . .

He looked at his reflection and analyzed himself. He had always gone to sea in order to escape the land. To sea to escape his original family, his drunken father and self-effacing mother. To sea to escape his second family, the one he had founded: the word "founded" seemed pretentious, because Greg had merely gone about possessing his legal wife, that was the whole point of marriage, no? He had sailed the world over: and yet he hadn't seen a thing. The freighter may have docked in any number of ports, Greg had gone no further on land than his ship had, he'd never left the pier, he put in his roots in the port, out of wariness, out of a fear of the unknown, a fear he might be left behind. Basically, in spite of the thousands of kilometers they had sailed, all the cities and nations and foreign landscapes were places he had imagined from on board the ship, or from the tavern on the pier, and they had all remained distant destinations.

As had his daughters. Exotic. Seen in passing. Nothing more.

What did he remember about Betty, the youngest? She was nine years old, a good student, and she lived in the attic room that Greg had reconverted into a bedroom. What else? He had trouble picturing her more precisely. He'd paid no attention to her desires, her aversions, her goals. Why hadn't he found the time to hang out with his daughters? The life he led was a rough one, he was nothing but a sort of beast of burden, an ox plowing the waves.

He looked one last time at the muscular body he'd been so proud of only a day earlier, then rinsed himself off and got dressed.

He continued to avoid any contact with the other men until

evening fell, and they respected what they presumed was his sorrow, not insisting at all, for they knew full well that Greg must be going through a crucifying ordeal. What they could not imagine was that his sorrow as a grieving father was compounded by the sorrow of being a bad father.

At midnight, beneath a sky as black as a dragon's mouth, on the planking where Greg was toiling at multiplying the pumps, Dexter asked, "So, we still don't know which one of your daughters . . . "

Greg almost replied, "It hardly matters, there's not one whom I know any better than the others," but merely grunted, "No."

"I have no idea how I'd react if something as horrible as that happened to me," murmured Dexter.

"Well, neither do I."

His reply had come out so pertinently that Dexter, who was not at all used to hearing Greg find the right words to express himself, was disconcerted.

Because Greg was experiencing an unexpected pain: he had begun to think. An incessant labor was taking shape inside him, a labor of reflection that exhausted him. He had not changed his skin, no, someone had found their way under his skin, another Greg was living inside the previous one, a psychological and intellectual consciousness was taking up residence in the once tranquil brute.

Back on his bunk he wept for a long time, without deliberating, without trying to determine who had died, and gradually he was overcome by weariness and closed his eyes. He fell asleep without even recovering the energy to get undressed or slide between the sheets, that deep, compact sleep which exhausts the sleeper and leaves him in the morning in a state of supreme irritation.

On waking he realized that ever since he had received the

fatal telegram he had not thought of his wife for an instant. Mary, moreover, was in his opinion no longer his wife but his family partner, his colleague with whom he was bringing up his daughters: he brought home the money, she put in her hours. That was it. Fair and square. Classic. He suddenly understood that she must be in pain, and that reminded him of the young girl he had met twenty years earlier . . . He realized that Mary, who was fragile and touching, must be overwhelmed with grief at this moment. How many years had it been since he told her he loved her? How many years since he had felt it? The thought was devastating.

The valves of anxiety had opened. Now he was thinking from morning to night, in an emotional whirlwind from night to morning, and it was painful, suffocating, extenuating.

With every passing hour he fretted over his daughters and his wife. Even when he was working there was a streak of sadness in his soul, a taste of bitterness, a melancholy which no manual activity could alleviate.

He spent the last afternoon of the return up on deck, leaning against a railing. Waves from the hull to the horizon, there was nothing to see, so he threw his head back and gazed at the sky. At sea one is drawn to the sky—it is more varied, richer, more changing than the waves, capricious like a woman. All sailors are in love with the clouds.

Greg's mind skipped from the contemplation of the light outside to his inner turmoil; he had never taken the opportunity to be like this, a man, a simple man, minute in the middle of the vast ocean, divided between the infinity of nature and the infinity of his thoughts.

As night his meditation ended in sobs.

Ever since he had received the telegram he had been aware that he was also the widower of the young woman that Mary had once been.

And in the course of these three days, the father who would

disembark the next day on the pier in Vancouver had lost all his daughters.

All of them. Not just one. Four.

The freighter would soon make landfall. Vancouver was visible on the horizon.

Lively, gracious seagulls swooped with precision, the true masters of a coast they knew better than any sailors, and which they could travel faster than any ship ever could.

On land, autumn was resplendent after a hot summer; the trees blazed in bright hues of yellow and orange; leaves were dying, sublimely, as if through these intense colors they were grateful for the surfeit of sunlight they would surrender all too soon.

The ship finally entered the port of Vancouver. Tall buildings, vigilant and erect, reflected in their windows the clouds and waves that bore the nostalgia of distant places. From one hour to the next the atmosphere changed, alternating between sun and rain in showers that the local inhabitants called "liquid sunshine."

The *Grandville* pulled alongside the pier with its towering derricks.

Greg was startled. He saw familiar figures along the dock. They were expecting him.

He counted, immediately. And saw his wife and three daughters, immediately.

One of them was missing.

He did not want to know which one, yet. He looked away and immersed himself in the mooring maneuver.

Once the ship was made fast he examined his mourning women, who stood in a row twenty meters below him, tiny yet distinct.

There it is.

Now he knows.

He knows who has died, and who is alive.

His heart bursts. On the one hand, a daughter has just been wrenched from him, and on the other, three of them have been restored to him. One has fallen but the others are reborn. Incapable of reacting, frozen, he feels like laughing, and he needs to cry.

Betty. So it was Betty, the youngest, the one he hardly had time to love.

The gangway is brought; he walks down.

But what is this? The moment he steps on land, Betty springs out of a box where she was hiding, and goes to join her sisters to hold their hands and greet their father.

How is this possible?

Standing frozen on the pavement, Greg counts: his four daughters are there before him, thirty strides away. He no longer understands a thing, he is paralyzed: his four daughters are alive. He clings to the ramp behind him, can no longer swallow his saliva. Was it a mistake, then? From the beginning . . . The telegram was not for him! It was meant for someone else. Yes, they had handed it to him when in fact it was destined for another sailor who had an only daughter. Death has spared his family!

Overjoyed, he runs up to them. He takes Mary in his arms and crushes her against him with a laugh. Surprised, she lets him stifle her. He has never embraced her with such warmth. Then he hugs his daughters several times, touching them, feeling them, checking that they are alive, he does not say a word, he cries out in happiness, his eyes mist over with emotion. Never mind. He's not ashamed anymore, he won't hide his tears—Greg, the modest, reserved, taciturn man; he kisses them, holds them tight, especially Joan, who trembles with astonishment. Every one of them seems like a miracle to him.

Finally he murmurs, "I am so happy to see you all again."

"Did they tell you?" asks his wife.

What is she talking about? Oh no, not her . . . Not her too . . . He doesn't want to be reminded of this absurd message anymore. He has banished it from his mind. It's none of his business. An error.

"What?"

"Dr. Simbadour assured me he had sent word to the ship."

Suddenly Greg freezes. What? Was the message in earnest? Was it really meant for him?

Mary looks down and says gravely, "I was in pain. I went to the hospital. A miscarriage. I lost our child."

Greg grasped what had eluded him earlier: his wife was pregnant at the time of his departure, he had forgotten. It was so unreal, the announcement of a child, when you couldn't even see the mother's belly getting round. Mary must have been expecting a daughter. If Dr. Simbadour didn't give the child's name, it was because the fetus didn't have one . . .

Mary and her four daughters were struck dumb by Greg's behavior in the days that followed. Not only did he look after his wife in a way he never had before, showering her with treasures of attentiveness, but he also insisted they baptize the little unborn girl.

"Rita. I am sure her name is Rita."

He said they must bury her. Every day he went to the cemetery with flowers; every day he cried over Rita's tiny grave, this child whom he had neither seen nor touched, and he whispered sweet words to her. Kate, Grace, Joan, and Betty would never have believed that this brute of a man could be capable of so much affection, attention, and delicacy. As they had nearly always spent time with an absent father, and their contact had been limited to his physical strength or orders they must obey, they now looked at him with a different eye and began to fear him a bit less.

When two months later Greg informed them that he had accepted a position as a longshoreman in the port, which meant he would no longer be going to sea, they were glad that this stranger, once so distant and dreaded, had become their father at last.

CONCERTO
TO THE MEMORY
OF AN ANGEL

It was while listening to Axel play the violin that Chris became aware of his own inferiority.

The notes of the concerto "To the Memory of an Angel" rose on the air, through the trees to the blue sky, the tropical mist, the trilling of birds, the lightness of clouds. Axel was not interpreting the piece, he was living it. He was inventing the melody; the changes of mood, shifts in pace, all came from him, and he carried the orchestra with him from one second to the next, using his fingers to create the melody that would convey his thoughts. His violin had become a voice, a voice that languished, hesitated, then found confidence and strength.

Chris succumbed to the charm of it, trying all the while to restrain himself, because he sensed there was danger: if he came to love Axel too deeply, he would despise his own self.

Ordinary musicians give the impression that they have walked in from the audience, merely left their seats to climb onto the stage, and most of the students who made up this festival orchestra were that sort of musician, with their tentative way of walking, their inexpensive eyeglasses, their hastily-chosen clothing. Axel, on the other hand, seemed to come from elsewhere, as if he had landed from some sublime planet where intelligence, taste, and elevated spirits reigned. He was of medium height, with a narrow waist, a smooth, proud chest, and a hypnotic, feline, triangular face framing immense eyes. His brown curls were light, carefree, youthful. Other boys with similarly harmonious and regular features might appear sad, or boring, because their expressions are empty; but Axel had an irrepressible energy about him. He was a young man of integrity and generosity, exuberant and severe at the same time, and he was as radiant as an idol, confident, at ease with the sublime, a willing accomplice to genius. As he played he meditated, with the incandescent authority conferred by inspiration; he accentuated the healing effect of the music, the way its spiritual dimension could make the listener a better person. His elbow moved with ease, his forehead was smooth, he embodied philosophy in a cantilena.

Chris fixed his gaze on his feet, annoyed. He had never played the piano to such perfection. Should he give it up? At the age of nineteen he already had a collection of medals, prizes, and certificates of excellence, and he was something of an ace at competitions, dealing easily with the sort of traps set for virtuosos, from Liszt to Rachmaninov; but now, confronted with this miracle called Axel, he realized that if he had a certain number of victories to his name it was because he had a rage in him, and was a hard worker. Chris knew only that which can be learned, whereas Axel knew that which cannot be learned. On a soloist's platform it is not enough to play correctly, one must also play with feeling; naturally Axel played with feeling, whereas Chris had only ever attained excellence through study, reflection, and imitation.

He shivered, despite the fact that the sun, on this island in Thailand, had driven the temperature to over thirty-five degrees. His shivering reflected his impatience: if only Axel would hurry up and stop inflicting this splendor upon him, and let the competition continue.

The workshop, entitled "Music and Sports in Winter," provided students from conservatories—gifted amateurs or future professionals—with an opportunity to combine leisure and physical activity with the advanced study of their instrument. Each of them had a private lesson with a professor for two hours a day, then met as a group for ensemble practice and sports. They could enjoy sailing, deep-sea diving, cycling, and running, and to mark the end of their stay, a rally was going to be held. The first prize was a week with the Berlin Philharmonic, one of the world's top orchestras.

Axel started on the second movement. Chris had always found this passage to be somewhat disparate, the composition not as strong, and he delighted in the thought that Axel might stumble, break the spell, and bore the audience. His hopes were in vain; Axel gave each note its color of indignation, rebellion, and fury, restoring shape and meaning to the piece. In the first movement Alban Berg's concerto evokes an "angel"—the dead child—but in the second, it describes the parents' sorrow.

"Unbelievable! He's better than any of the recommended recordings."

How could this twenty-year old boy surpass artists like Ferras, Grumiaux, Menuhin, Perlman, and Stern?

The concerto came to a sublime close, the tip of the bow evoking a chorale by Bach, delivering the last-minute conviction that there is a reason for everything, even tragedy—an astonishing profession of faith for a modernist composer, but one which Axel managed to make as convincing as it was moving.

The audience applauded wildly, as did the members of the orchestra, tapping against their music stands. The young Australian musician was embarrassed, for he thought he had been self-effacing, in the service of Alban Berg alone, and he could not understand why they were applauding him; he was a mere performer. So he acknowledged them, awkwardly, but even his awkwardness had something graceful about it.

Chris rose to his feet to applaud along with his neighbors, and he bit his lip as he looked around him: this violinist had even managed to arouse the enthusiasm of an ignorant public—bathers, beach attendants, locals—for a dodecaphonic piece of music! By the third curtain call, Chris was beginning to find Axel's exploit unbearable, so he slipped through the excited crowd, leaving the concert hall that had been hastily set up among the palm trees, and headed for his tent.

On his way he ran into Paul Brown, the gentleman from New York who organized these international sessions.

"Well, did my little Cortot enjoy the concert?"

Paul Brown called Chris his little Cortot because Chris was a pianist, and French; for American academics Cortot was the quintessence of a French pianist.

"Axel has made me discover a work that normally I'm not at all keen on!"

"You seem almost annoyed—do you feel pushed to the point you want to lay down your arms? It's as if you were not at all pleased to find yourself liking Berg or admiring Axel."

"Admiration is not my strong point. I prefer a challenge: competition and victory."

"I know. You two are opposites, you and Axel. One smiles, the other sweats. You're a fighter, he's Zen. You view life as a struggle, while Axel just goes along never imagining there could ever be the slightest danger."

Paul Brown eyed Chris closely. Nineteen years of age, dark eyes, a wild head of hair, all the pride of a pampered son. He had a solid, sturdy body and wore a pair of poet's eyeglasses and a manly pointed beard, trimmed with scissors, as if he were seeking to be treated with all the respect owed to maturity.

"And who's right?" asked Chris.

"I'm afraid you are."

"Ah . . ."

"Yes, I know I'm American for a reason, my little Cortot. Innocence and confidence are fine, but not much use in our world. Talent may be a prerequisite for starting off a career, but to get somewhere you have to have ambition and fierce determination. You have the right attitude."

"Ah! And in your opinion, do I play better than Axel?"

"I didn't say that. No one will play better than Axel. On the other hand I imagine that you will have a greater career than he will."

There was a considerable amount of reservation in his remark, even condemnation, but Chris decided to retain only the compliment. Tapping himself on the forehead, Paul Brown cried out, amused, "Cain and Abel! If I were to rename the two of you, that's what I'd suggest. Two brothers with completely opposite characteristics: Cain the tough guy, and Abel the gentle soul."

Delighted with himself, the American rounded his mouth and looked at Chris, waiting for his reaction. Chris merely shrugged his shoulders and called out, as he went on his way, "Let's just keep to 'little Cortot,' if you don't mind. And I hope the 'little' only refers to my age . . . "

On the morning of the last Sunday Chris bounded out of bed impatiently, his hair standing upright on his head: to sleep was impossible, he needed action, he could feel his muscles itching for a confrontation.

The night before, he had worried that he might miss the closing rally because his mother had informed him that he had an audition on Tuesday morning with some important Parisian program planners. The wise thing would have been to leave at once, the moment he got the news, because he had to reach the coast by boat, then make his way to Bangkok—four hours by road—before stewing for twelve hours on a long haul flight to go halfway round the globe; even supposing he did leave right away, he would never have time to recover from the jetlag in France. So Chris rejected the common sense solution, took another look at the timetables of the connections and managed, rather acrobatically, to justify his presence at the rally by proving that he could take the ferryboat on Sunday evening.

Why put himself through so much stress? He wasn't really interested in the prize, because for a pianist an entire week with an orchestra, even the Berlin Philharmonic, would not provide him with many opportunities to perform; no, it was because he was eager for combat, to challenge Axel and defeat him. He would not leave his Australian rival until he had proven that he was better; he wanted to make him bite the dust.

At breakfast, he swung his leg over the bench and sat down opposite the violinist, who looked up at him.

"Hi, Chris," exclaimed Axel, "glad to see you."

Axel smiled, and there was a vague tenderness about him, something to do with the shape of his eyelids and his almost feminine abandonment, an air which regularly left girls broken-hearted and men feeling disconcerted. At the same time, his wide open blue eyes often focused on other people, and it was as if they were being subjected to an X-ray rather than a mere gaze.

"Hi, Axel. Working up an appetite for today?"

"Why? What's on today? Oh, right, the rally . . . "

When he laughed, he threw his head back, showing his neck, as if he expected to be kissed.

Chris could not imagine why Axel was not more excited about the competition. "He's making fun of me! He's pretending to be relaxed but in actual fact he only got out of bed for that very reason."

"I wonder," continued Axel, "whether I should go. All I feel like doing this afternoon is going down to the beach to do some reading, I've got some scores and a book to finish."

"You can't go off and leave everyone like that!" protested Chris. "They might have liked your playing as a soloist, but they might take it badly if you go off on your own."

Axel blushed.

"You're right, forgive me, I'll join in. Thanks for putting me back on track. Sometimes I behave in a really monstrous way, I tend to think only about myself instead of the group."

To himself Chris grumbled, "Think about me, in particular, because you're going to get a hiding from me."

The contest began at nine o'clock. The candidates were all given a bike, a map of the island, and a first clue; after the starting signal they had to go from marker to marker, finding the clues that led from one marker to the next, until they reached the last place where the treasure was hidden. Whoever broke into the pirate's chest first would grab the coin with the number one, the next in line would be number two, and so on.

"May the best man win!" shouted Paul Brown, red in the face, the veins in his neck bulging.

A loud bang resounded in the turquoise sky.

Chris set off, with all the energy of a final sprint, thinking hard as he pedaled and elbowed his way past his neighbors.

By the third stage he was at the head of the pack. Solving the rebuses and locating the hiding places were child's play to him, yet he was not about to relent or let up on the pressure.

There was a first annoying detail: two participants were hot on his heels, Bob and Kim, from Texas and Korea respectively. He thought with a moan, "I'm not in this competition to have two guys like that as my rivals! A tuba player and a percussionist!" Like all musicians, Chris had established a hierarchy: at the top were the great soloists—pianists, violinists and cellists; then came flautists, viola players, harpists and assorted clarinetists; at the bottom were the menial drudges who played poor, limited instruments that provided mere background noise, like tubas and percussion.

"Why is Axel so far behind in the pack?"

He tried to understand his rival through his own self, and concluded that Axel must be going slowly on purpose, taking part half-heartedly to avoid the confrontation with Chris; by competing at a slower pace Axel could always find the excuse that if he had wanted to, he would have won.

"Bastard! Cheater! Loser!" hissed Chris, weaving back and forth on his bike as he climbed a steep slope.

When he came to the tenth clue, he turned around and saw that Axel had caught up with Bob and Kim.

"Ah-hah, now he's at it."

The mettle of one's adversaries determines the worthiness of a competition and sets the price of the victory: when Chris saw Axel on his heels, he felt a sudden boost of energy.

Despite the fact that the sun was at its zenith, he put all his mental and physical strength to work for the final stages. The increasing difficulty of the riddles had slowed Kim and Bob down, and left the rest of the group far behind; before long the only ones still in front were the Australian and Chris himself. At last the race was turning into the duel that Chris had hoped for.

"Duel, duet . . . That old jerk Pastella in chamber music said I was mixing up the two! 'A duet means playing together, Mr. Chris; a duel is playing one against the other,' the old loser used to say over and over. It's no surprise he ended up rotting away in a teaching position, without ever confronting an audience—he never figured it out that everything, always, is a duel!"

Besides, wasn't that what happened last Wednesday, when Paul Brown asked Axel and Chris to perform César Franck's Sonata for Violin and Piano? After a few bars, when Chris realized that Axel was performing the piece as easily and freshly as if he had composed it himself that very morning, he decided he must divert the listeners' attention by showing the range of his mastery of the piano—increasing the nuances, accentuating the contrasts, now lively, now tender and dreamy, now seething, excessive, and mannered, all according to the needs of the score; Chris was knowingly over-interpreting Franck's work so that Axel's contribution would seem timid and lifeless in comparison. And it worked: Chris was showered with compliments. Only Paul Brown frowned skeptically to convey to his French student that he knew what he was trying to do and didn't like it one bit.

The twentieth marker! From the symbols, Chris had concluded that the treasure must be underwater, beneath a mass of coral. At last he'd be able to make good use of his months of training.

Four minutes ahead of Axel, he reached the coast, hid his bike behind a bush then ran to the inlet indicated on his map.

There a hut was waiting with diving gear bearing the logo "Music and Sports in Winter."

"Perfect, I was dead on."

Every ten seconds he glanced furtively over his shoulder to check that he was still ahead as he adjusted his suit, strapped the bottle onto his back, stepped into his flippers and pulled down the mask.

Suddenly Axel appeared. Chris rushed into the water as if he'd been stung; determined to be first, he glided toward the coral with long kicks of his flippers.

"According to my calculations, it must be to the east."

On he went, in smooth undulations on the surface. Instinctively, after he'd gone a hundred meters, he turned around to see where Axel was: he had just headed off to the west.

"West? Why is he headed west?"

If it had been anyone else, Chris wouldn't have paid any attention, but given Axel's discernment, doubt began to needle its way into his teeming thoughts.

Kicking his legs, he deliberated, reworked the puzzle of clues and suddenly stopped.

"He's right!"

Furious, he turned abruptly and lengthened his strokes, trying to gain speed, frightened fishes fleeing all around him. He might still be lucky, because Axel was hugging the rocks, while he was cutting straight across the water.

Near the coral reef, well away from the liquid lagoon, Chris thought he could see an unusual shape. Was it the chest? He moved faster, despite the risk of straining a muscle or losing air.

To the right of him, Axel was making his way along the coral wall, then he slid into an enormous massif with sharp ridges. Was it some dangerous creature that caused him to recoil abruptly? Did he feel a sudden malaise? Did he lean against a loose rock without realizing it? A first block gave way, and then a second, and Axel's form vanished in a cloud of debris.

Chris hesitated. What should he do? Go over to him? Help him? That is what he had been taught when he took his diving permit. At the same time, he wanted to be sure that the brown spot over on his left, at a depth of ten meters, was indeed the pirate chest.

To obey the code all the same, he headed toward the troubled waters where Axel was wriggling. Axel's feet were trapped in a fissure by the rockslide. When he saw Chris, he waved his arms, signaling distress.

"Okay, okay, I'll come and help you," motioned Chris, "but first I'm going over there to get the proof that I've won, the number one coin."

Axel protested, rolling his eyes, increasing his gestures for help.

No way, old man, I'm not playing that game! thought Chris, veering off to the left. I know the trick: as soon as I help you, you'll break free, push me, and rush off to steal the number one coin. Besides, you're right, I can't hold it against you, I'd do the same thing. But insofar as I have a choice, I'll help myself first. See you later, number two.

As he moved away he could see Axel was now waving frantically, grimacing with fear, shouting soundlessly fit to drown.

Oh, that's normal, thought Chris with a laugh as he glanced over at his rival. The thought of losing just makes him hysterical. Taking his time, with some difficulty Chris lifted the heavy lid covering the pieces of brass, found the one which said Number One, put it in the pocket of his diving suit, then slowly turned to go back to Axel.

When he was a few meters away he saw there was something wrong: the bubbles were coming out of Axel's back and not his mask, and his body was no longer wriggling. What was going on? A shiver of fear went through him. What if the oxygen hose had been severed by the rockslide? Overcome by panic, Chris gave a few quick, powerful kicks with his flippers. Too late: Axel was motionless, his eyelids closed, his mouth gaping, lifeless. The rocks crushing his feet kept him prisoner of the depths.

At that moment, Chris saw a shadow in the distance. It was Kim, searching along the sea bed for the last marker.

Chris had to think quickly: either he stayed here, and he would have to explain why he hadn't helped Axel sooner; or he had to swim discreetly away and leave Kim to discover the corpse.

Without further ado he went deeper into the reef so that Kim would not see him; anyway, for the time being Kim was going off in the wrong direction. Chris made his way to the beach, hid behind some palm trees, removed his diving gear and kept an eye on both the sea and the land, where he feared he might see another participant emerge from the water at any moment.

Then he ran to his bike, congratulating himself for having hidden it out of sight: Kim would not be able to claim that Chris had been anywhere near there, and he pedaled away like crazy. Breathless, his heart pounding fit to burst, he went back to base camp and crossed the finish line, victorious.

His fellow students who hadn't taken part in the rally or

who had given up along the way offered their congratulations. Paul Brown, his armpits squelchy, his forehead streaming with sweat, and his pale redhead's skin now bright crimson from the sun, came forward with a smile.

"Well done, Chris. I'm not surprised. I hesitated whether to place my bet on you or Axel."

"Thank you."

"Who's behind you?"

"I don't know. The last time I looked it was Kim. At one point I saw Axel getting closer, but then he fell back. As far as I can tell, Kim and Axel were fighting for second place, but they were far behind. During the final leg, when I left the inlet, neither one of them had reached it yet."

He gave an inner bow to his clever ruse: he had told a pretty little fib that would lend credence to his absence from the site of the rockslide and free him from any responsibility. Paul nodded and waved to one of his assistants to bring the luggage.

"You know, my little Cortot, that you have to leave soon, and maybe even before the others come back?"

"I know. Why do you think I got here first?"

"Take your bags, the boat's waiting. Well done, as I said. I wish you all the best for your future. You'll have a fine career, no need for me to insist on the fact, because I know you will."

He gave the young man a big American hug, holding him close and tapping him on the back with his hands. Chris was disgusted by the man's flabby belly and decided that when he was Paul's age he would forbid himself from putting on weight.

"Delighted to have met you, Chris."

"Delighted, Paul . . . delighted."

He was in such a hurry to get away that even echoing what Paul had said made him feel awkward.

In the hours that followed, on the boat, in the Jeep, and on the plane, Chris could not stop ruminating, poisoned by the same two or three thoughts: he must double-check the solidity of his plan, respond to any objections, imagine the worst-case scenario and come up with a way to get out of it. It was not that he was particularly concerned about Axel; he thought only about himself, and himself alone—the fact that he might be guilty, or what others, in bad faith, might reproach him with.

When Chris landed in Paris, that 4th of December 1980, he hadn't slept a wink, but by the time he had made it through customs without any questions, he figured he was safe. "No one will come after me here, and it's all behind me. Hurrah!" He ran off to the toilets to dance with joy, as if he had just won the competition all over again.

He waited by the conveyor belt as it spat out the baggage, and looked all around him with a kindly gaze, as if he were meeting an old friend. He was delighted by the huge white walls, the marble floor, the immaculate chrome, the openwork ceiling filtering the mercurial light of Paris. Suddenly, on the far side of the high glass walls in the arrivals hall he saw his mother. She was looking desperately all around her, anxious that he might be late, worried that she could not see her only child. Such distress! And so much love contained in her anguish . . .

He shuddered.

In Sydney there was a mother with the same distraught face who was about to learn that her son was gone forever.

The clarity of it was devastating: Chris now understood that Axel had just died and that he, Chris, was his assassin.

*

In that month of June 2001, Mr. and Mrs. Beaumont, vendors of religious items, were absolutely delighted to find themselves staying in Shanghai.

They could not help but look up repeatedly, their eyes darting full of wonder from the teak table piled high with goods, through the slightly smoked display window, and out onto the teeming Chinese city: twenty million inhabitants spreading as far as the eye could see, a jumble of tenements and tall buildings bristling with antennas, cluttered with advertising ideograms; a steaming, mineral forest where skyscrapers slashed like swords at the clouds.

"Do you see, darling, that shiny building over there in the shape of a rocket? It must be at least fifty floors, don't you think?"

"At least," confirmed Mrs. Beaumont.

Miss Mee, speaking a fruity French of short, sweet sounds, called the two merchants to order. "May I please go back over your list, Sir? Madam?"

"Go ahead," said Beaumont to his supplier, like a king who is being served.

"Go," insisted Mrs. Beaumont, who was in the habit of repeating one word from her husband's last sentence in order not to annoy him.

Taking up her notebook, Miss Mee stabbed her pen at each line of the order with the authority of a head pupil.

"So, you have chosen the St. Rita Keychain on special offer (15,000 in metal, 15,000 in epoxy), the St. Rita license plate (4,000 units), the rosary with twenty-two beads and a medallion with the Saint's effigy (50,000), as well as the mug (4,000), the egg cup (4,000), the candlesticks (5,000), and the bowls (10,000). And at the trial price of one dollar per item I will throw in one hundred St. Rita terrycloth bibs for hopelessly dirty babies. Now, can I tempt you with a superb St. Rita statuette, six centimeters high, to put in the car? The adhesive base means you can stick it anywhere."

"How much?"

"Four dollars. A low price but fantastic quality. It's silver plated metal."

Miss Mee placed a special emphasis on "silver plated metal," as if she were informing them it was pure silver.

"Add one thousand, we sometimes come across truck drivers who are very religious," said Mr. Beaumont.

"And what about St. Rita badges?"

"Nobody buys badges anymore in France."

Mrs. Beaumont suddenly squealed, "And what about pill-boxes?"

"Pill . . . what?" asked Miss Mee, who was unfamiliar with the expression.

"Pillboxes! For sick people! The followers of St. Rita, patron saint of the impossible, are often undergoing medical treatment. In my opinion, they would snap up pillboxes."

"Add 40,000, Miss Mee. And that should do it."

Miss Mee handed them the order form, which Mr. Beaumont signed, crimson, aware of its importance.

"Might we have the honor of saying hello to Mr. Lang?"

"Of course," said Miss Mee, "since the president promised you."

"We've been his clients for so long . . . " said Mr. Beaumont. "It will be a pleasure to shake Mr. Lang's hand."

"The mysterious Mr. Lang," whispered Mrs. Beaumont.

Miss Mee refrained from responding; in her opinion there was nothing mysterious about Mr. Lang, her boss; on the contrary, he was clearly the biggest bastard she had ever known.

She called the president's secretary, then left the Beaumonts in the room.

As the Beaumonts stood gazing out at the panorama, a man came in the room behind them.

"Hello," said a shrill voice.

The Beaumonts turned around, prepared to offer effusive greetings, but were stopped short by the sight of the individual looking them up and down from his wheelchair.

Mr. Lang was dressed in dark colors, his clothes were smudged with greasy stains and a three day beard exacerbated his unhealthy complexion. He hid his eyes behind dark glasses, his hair—what remained of it—beneath a shapeless hat, and his emotions—if he had any—behind an impenetrably hard mask. He maneuvered the electric chair with his left hand, and it was impossible to know what had happened to his legs or his right arm, merely that they were thin, twisted, and completely stiff. He was not a man, but a scribble of a man—a draft, a sketch, a botched creature.

"Would you like me to show you around our workshops?"

Repulsed, Mrs. Beaumont thought he must be doing it on purpose, yes, deliberately speaking in that squeaky, toneless voice, as unpleasant as a fingernail scratching against a windowpane. She grabbed her husband's upper arm and dug her fingers in.

"Would you like that?" insisted Lang, annoyed by the French couple's silence.

Mr. Beaumont started as if he had suddenly woken up.

"With pleasure."

"Pleasure . . . " mumbled Mrs. Beaumont.

Mr. Lang immediately rolled toward the elevator, inviting them to follow. The Beaumonts looked at each other. They were chilled, overcome by a diffuse malaise, and they could no longer behave normally. They felt none of the warm pity normally triggered by the sight of an invalid; in Lang they sensed such raging hostility that they could not help but reproach him for his infirmity, accuse him for having added this provocation to his arsenal, as if it were a deliberate aggression, a refined form of insolence.

In the basement Lang burst out of the elevator, furious at having had to share his air for twenty-five floors with these tourists, and he pointed to the neon-lit workshop where a hundred or more Chinese workers were busy at their tasks.

"This is where we manufacture our products."

"Why St. Rita?" asked Mr. Beaumont with unctuous kindness.

He gave a victorious wink to his wife because he was convinced that his clever question would give Mr. Lang the opportunity to explain the cause of his infirmity and, in so doing, he might become a bit more human.

Mr. Lang answered straight off the bat.

"There was a niche for it."

"I beg your pardon?"

"Yes, Jesus and the Virgin Mary dominate the market. In Europe, saints are no longer in fashion, except for St. Rita and St. Jude, if you market them properly."

"St. Jude?"

Mr. and Mrs. Beaumont had never heard about St. Jude or sold any items representing him. Lang grumbled, impatient with his clients' ignorance.

"The parking saint! Call on St. Jude and he'll help you find a place to park: since he's not very well-known, he has time to take care of you. And he fixes things very quickly."

"Is that so? Does it really work?"

"You must be joking! I'm just telling you what you have to say in order to sell him. Didn't Miss Mee tell you about St. Jude?"

"No."

"What an idiot! She'll be out the door first thing tomorrow."

Mrs. Beaumont went bright red when she saw what a worker was removing from a mold before her very eyes.

"But . . . but . . . but . . . "

"Yes, we also manufacture these," said Mr. Lang approvingly. "Pornographic accessories. Are you interested?"

Mr. Beaumont went up to the plastic phallus set amidst a number of silicon women's buttocks.

"Oh! How repulsive."

"You're mistaken," said Lang, "they are excellent items, as good as our religious accessories. Once you have the actual casts, you know, you use the same materials and the same techniques."

"It's an insult! To think that our St. Ritas come into the world next to these . . . these . . . "

"As does St. Rita, and all the rest of us, sir! You are only a wholesaler for religious items? It's a pity, because once you're in the business . . . "

The telephone rang. Lang listened, did not speak, hung up, and then paying no further attention to the Beaumonts he said, "I'm going back up."

The French couple hardly had time to say goodbye before the doors of the elevator closed behind Lang.

As soon as he got to his office, he rushed over to his secretary, a young Korean man of twenty-five years of age, tall and thin as a reed.

"Well?"

"They have found him, sir."

For the very first time, the secretary saw his boss smile: Mr. Lang's mouth opened and a short laugh came from his throat.

"At last!"

Certain of pleasing the tyrant, the secretary provided the information he had at his disposal: "He doesn't work in the field we were investigating. You said it was classical music, did you not?"

"Yes, what does he do? Has he gone over to pop music?"

"This activity has nothing to do with art. Here's a leaflet about the place where he works."

Mr. Lang grabbed the folded paper. He was ordinarily so impenetrable, but now he could not help but raise his eyebrows, marking a moment of astonishment.

"And you're sure it's him?"

"Absolutely."

Lang nodded.

"I want to go there. Immediately. Book me on the next flight."

The secretary stepped behind the desk and picked up the telephone. While he was dialing the number, Lang said carelessly, "Get rid of Miss Mee at once, tonight. Professional incompetence."

The secretary reached their travel agency.

"I'd like to book a flight to France. The town of Annecy . . . No direct flights? Are you sure? He has to go Shanghai-Paris, then Paris-Grenoble, then rent a car for Annecy? Or Shanghai-Geneva and go the rest of the way by taxi?"

He held his palm over the receiver and asked his boss, "Is that all right with you, sir?"

The nabob of religious and pornographic artifacts nodded his head.

"All right," continued the secretary. "Shanghai-Geneva. As soon as possible. In business. The name is Lang. Axel Lang."

Making his way to the window where the light was better, Axel took the leaflet his secretary had given him and turned it this way and that, trying to make out on the tiny photographs the face of the man he had been trying to find for months, and whose memory had been dogging him for twenty years.

Sunil, his physiotherapist, a fleshy giant and former judo champion, interrupted him with a clap of his hands.

"Time for your session, sir."

A few minutes later Axel, his skin oiled, was receiving the daily care his rehabilitation necessitated. He had placed the leaflet beneath the open space in the massage table for the eyes and nose, and he was now learning it by heart, humming to himself.

"You seem to be in a better mood than usual, Mr. Lang."

What business is that of his, moron? grumbled Axel to himself. Why should he care whether I'm happy today or in a bad mood on other days? He's a masseur, not a psychiatrist, jerk!

Five minutes later Axel was humming again, and the former

judoka, in a surge of friendliness, took the liberty of repeating his question, presuming that his patient would be in the mood to share his emotions.

"What is making you so happy, Mr. Lang?"

"A promise. I swore to myself that once I earned my first billion, I would make a dream come true. My dream."

"Ah, really? Congratulations, sir. On the first billion, I mean."

"You're hurting me, idiot."

"Forgive me. And what is your dream, sir?"

"To go to France."

"That I can understand . . . "

"To Annecy."

"Hmm, never heard of it."

"Me neither. To the Villa Socrates."

"The Villa Socrates? What's that?" asked the masseur with a drawl. "A restaurant? Thalassotherapy? A high end clinic?"

"None of that. Simply the place where I am going to get my revenge. I'm hesitating between torture and murder."

"Very funny, Mr. Lang!"

The huge man's laugh rang hollow; there was more stupidity than joy in his sudden outburst. Axel, who had been getting massages from Sunil for over six months, now thought that he could no longer put up with the former wrestler's serenity, his mindless conversation and damp hands. Tomorrow, before he left, he would fire him.

Pacified, he looked again at the photographs in the leaflet, where adults were posing, gripping each other's shoulders. Where was he? Which one of these men was he? What might Chris look like now?

*

Strains of the concerto "To the Memory of an Angel" emerged discreetly, timidly, furtively from the loudspeakers. A memory of music more than a living music. In his room under the eaves, Chris was careful never to increase the volume because in this large wooden house perched on the mountainside sounds traveled from room to room; he wouldn't want one of the adolescents he looked after at the Villa Socrates to come up and attack him, criticizing his taste—not that he was ashamed of it, but because this particular work belonged to his private life, and he did not share his private life with anyone.

The stereo was a cheap one—the sound crackled, the violin was a mere line, the orchestra a muddle of sound, just enough to give him an idea of the work and set his memories loose. Chris listened to this CD the way you might look at a slide with faded colors; the music was a prop for his reverie.

Since Axel's death he had not been able to stop thinking about him. In the beginning it was a tiny spring, a trickle of water in his memory, but over time the stream had swollen to the size and strength of a river. Arrested in his genius, his kindness, his perfection, Axel now occupied an essential place in Chris's spirit—he was an icon, a saint, virtually a god to whom Chris the atheist would turn whenever he had a dilemma.

Chris would sit on his chair behind the little desk where the light of day fell and contemplate his favorite vision of the countryside as it changed from season to season. Through the dormer window you could see more of water and sky than of land. A window open upon infinity? At the bottom of the hill the lake of Annecy slept beneath a pure sky where eagles circled. On the slopes of the opposite shore the houses among the fir trees looked like cobblestones in a dark meadow, while higher up, herds of white mountain peaks grazed ghostly in the distance.

"Hey, Chris, come quickly, we have a problem."

Laura, a colleague who looked terribly thin in her Lolita jeans and loose T-shirt, had come into the room.

He followed her. Without saying a word, so that their

boarders would not hear them, they hurried into the director's office, the only isolated room in the chalet.

Montignault, the founder of the villa, gathered his seven instructors around him and said, "Karim, our newest arrival, has run away. No sign of him this morning in either his bed, the workshop, or the barn."

"We have to inform the gendarmerie!" exclaimed Laura.

Montignault frowned.

"Let's leave that as late as we can, Laura, first we'll have a look. It's not a good idea to send the gendarmes after a kid who has already spent far too much time with the police in his previous life. He'll only find a better way to hide, or he'll attack them, or if they catch him he'll despise us and assimilate us with the cops. That would be counterproductive. We'd lose any influence over him."

The group agreed, including Laura. In this center devoted to troubled adolescents—drugs, victims of violence or rape, pre-delinquents—the instructors, who cared passionately about their work, did not nurture their own egos and were able to admit as much when they were wrong. The children mattered more than they did.

"I imagine that some of you might have established closer ties with him. Who knows him a little?"

Chris raised his hand.

"Yes, Chris. Give us some clues."

"I'm afraid he may not have run away."

"What do you mean?" asked Montignault worriedly.

"Karim has suicidal tendencies."

A dismayed silence greeted his words. The special needs teachers sat down around the office and thought through the ways in which Karim might attempt to put an end to his life.

Twenty minutes later Chris was headed toward the railroad line below the Villa Socrates. In order to determine which way to go, he tried to put himself in Karim's place: here was a boy who had been brought up in an underprivileged neighborhood. Since a death wish is a sign of regression, an act that aims to regain the comfort of childhood, the young man must have found a place in this Alpine landscape—utterly exotic to him—that would remind him of his original slum in the outskirts of Paris. What could be more universal than the railroad? The same smell in the country as in the town, a mixture of coal, oil, and organic waste. The same signs above steel bars. The same danger, were a locomotive suddenly to appear.

Chris followed the narrow river as it rippled and foamed and flowed over its bed of stones, where here and there a tuft of green grass waved. An icy wind slapped his face. No doubt about it, winter would soon be here.

When he came alongside the tracks, Chris looked in both directions: no one.

He suddenly remembered that farther along there was something else that might attract the kid: an overpass above the railroad line. As he recalled the location, Chris shed any further doubts: Karim must be there, waiting for a train to come, to fling himself beneath the wheels.

At a run, careful not to be seen, he covered the kilometer leading to the place. Spot on! He could see a figure on the overpass looking out at the horizon.

He approached Karim from behind, and only began to speak to him when he was a few inches away.

"Karim, I think this morning you're hurting all over."

The adolescent swung around, hesitating between his fury at being found, his surprise at seeing Chris, the instructor he had befriended, and the emotion caused by his words.

"You are hurting, is that it, it hurts?" said Chris again gently.

Karim wanted to say yes, but to say yes would have been giving an answer, and he didn't want to answer anybody.

"It's your life, Karim, you can do what you want with it."

To the rebellious boy it was as if Chris had just read his mind.

"I don't want to spoil your decision, or the time you're spending here. The problem is that I am going to stay with you, and if the train comes along, I will stop you from jumping. So yeah, I can see I'm a nuisance."

Karim turned away, disturbed by so much understanding.

"Let me make a suggestion, Karim: why don't I buy you a drink up there?"

He pointed to an auberge some ways above them, tiny yet visible, a red dot in the middle of the steep slope.

"Let's go have a chat up there. And after that you can do what you like."

"I'll come back here!" shouted Karim, as if to prove that he was not some indecisive weakling.

"Okay," concluded Chris. "If you want, you can come back here and I'll leave you alone. But first, come and have a coffee or a hot chocolate with me."

"You swear you'll leave me alone afterwards?"

"I swear."

Once the boy was sure his touchy pride had been respected, he shoved his hands into his pockets, hunched his shoulders and lowered his head, all of which meant, "I'm coming."

From the terrace of the inn, higher up, a man had been watching the scene with considerable interest. When he saw that the two figures were coming toward him, he turned his wheelchair and headed back inside to come to a stop between two columns, in a place where he hoped he would not be noticed.

They came into the room with red checked curtains and tablecloths, cowbells decorating the windowsills. Karim was only convinced it was a café once he saw the espresso maker behind the zinc counter and the pinball machine near the door to the toilets.

Chris ordered two hot chocolates and they curled their frozen palms around the stoneware bowls before they drank.

"Why do you want to do away with yourself?"

"Because I'm good for nothing. All I do is screw up."

"How old are you?"

"Sixteen."

"Well, let's just say you've been screwing up until the age of sixteen. Afterwards, you—"

"What are you talking about! If you're made of iron, you stay iron. If you're made of wood, you stay wood. If you're made of shit, like me, you stay shit."

"That's not true. You can change. I'm the proof of it."

"You? You've always been like this!"

"Oh yeah? I've always been like this, some sort of St. Bernard who thinks about others before thinking about himself? It so happens that when I was your age I couldn't give a damn about other people, I walked all over them, I thought about no one but myself."

"You're just saying that to—"

"I'm just saying that because it's true. We don't stay bad forever, Karim, if we become aware of it, we can improve. We are free, Karim, free!"

"Free, me? As soon as I'm old enough to go to jail that's where they'll put me. And they'll be right. I don't want to stick around to see it."

"You don't believe in redemption?"

"What you talking about?"

Six feet away, hanging on every word, Axel was finding it harder and harder to breathe. He withdrew further into his hiding place to eavesdrop.

"You can change your destiny, Karim. A thief can become an honest man, a murderer can come to realize that he has done wrong and never do it again. Karim, you may have started out with vandalism, pillaging, break-ins and dealing in heroin, but that doesn't mean you can't learn to behave well. The proof is that you disgust your own self. A really bad person thinks he is good. Just as a real jerk doesn't even know he's a jerk. You see, you've already moved up to the next category. I have faith in you, Karim. You have my word, I will help you all the way if I can."

They fell silent. Karim warmed himself with the hot chocolate, but also with Chris's words.

To avoid appearing sentimental, to keep strong—according to his criteria—he maintained his rebellious stance: "Who are you? Why do you care what happens to me? You're not my brother!"

"Not directly."

"What's that supposed to mean?"

"That I can feel like your brother even if I'm not your blood brother."

"Bozo! You can only be brothers through blood, and the rest is just bull."

"Oh really? Because you've never seen brothers fighting or hating each other in your neighborhood? And what about you and your family, what have your brothers done for you?"

"They're too little, I'm the oldest."

"And you want to do away with yourself. Smart move, the ideal older brother!"

"That's enough . . . it's my business what I do."

"Exactly. Do you know the story of the two brothers, Cain and Abel?"

"Sure, it's in the Koran."

"In the Bible, too. They were the sons of Adam and Eve and they lived together without a hitch until the famous quarrel about the offerings. Abel gave God the products of his activity as a breeder—no doubt an ox and sheep—while Cain, as a farmer, offered fruit and vegetables. Now God for no apparent reason accepted Abel's gift but refused Cain's. You know life can be that way, unfair, unpredictable, never the same. You just have to accept it. So Cain, who was very proud, didn't accept it, went into a rage and rebelled. God told him off and advised him to calm down. No way! In a fit of rage Cain killed his brother Abel because he was jealous. At the scene of the crime, but too late, God asked him why. Cain just laughed and said, 'Am I my brother's keeper?' Well yes, he was, but he didn't realize that, he hadn't thought about the great human family. Every man is responsible for every other man, for his brother and all the others. If you kill someone, it means you're forgetting that. If you're violent, you're forgetting. I don't want to forget anymore: I am your keeper, Karim, and I won't let you down. And you are the keeper of your little brothers: not only must you not abandon them, but you must help them, too."

"Okay . . . and then what?"

"God sent Cain far away to a land where he had to work; he was eaten away by guilt, and he had children; all humanity up until Noah is said to stem from his descendents. Which goes to show that violence doesn't stop you from getting ahead. And, above all, that there is no life without violence, you just have to learn to restrain it."

"When I said, 'and then what?' I wasn't talking about Cain, I was talking about myself!"

"You come back with me, you trust me, and you trust yourself. Maybe you will turn into the person you really are, the real Karim, not the Karim the hoods in your neighborhood have turned you into."

"Do you believe in God?"

"No. But I like stories that make me feel less alone and less stupid."

"Well I do, I do believe in God!" said Karim, proud to express his conviction and superiority.

Chris could tell he had won from Karim's attitude: the kid would not go back to throw himself under a train.

Shortly afterwards they left the room, close together, so that at times their shoulders touched, and they took the path back to Villa Socrates.

Axel strained to follow them with his gaze until they vanished in the distance. "Disappointed," was the only word that drifted through his mind—"disappointed," yes, "profoundly disappointed," because he could never have imagined he would see Chris again behaving and speaking like this.

He, too, had the impression he had changed.

Where was the jubilation he had expected to feel? Why was he no longer enchanted by the proximity of vengeance? Where was the black joy he had felt at the mere thought that he was about to strike? It was time to get a grip . . .

With its huge bay windows, the pool had been designed to give the illusion of swimming in the midst of Alpine nature, where meadows sloped down from the peaks to the lake on the valley floor, all beneath the peaceful gaze of snow-capped mountains. But on that day the pool seemed to be cut off from the world by a thick wall of steam that clung to the glass, warm droplets lured by the cold air to block any view of the valley.

In the main pool a few swimmers were doing laps, moving smoothly across the expanse, unconcerned by others. An old insect-like man with a swollen belly over his rickety legs stood next to the diving board making slow circles with his arms.

A hairless lifeguard with thick soft thighs sat on a high chair overlooking the entire facility, with his whistle between his lips like some outsize baby sucking on a bottle.

An employee had pushed Axel's chair as far as the small pool; wrapped in a dressing gown he now sat observing the man who had become his obsession.

Chris was in the water attending to an elderly woman with rheumatism. He held her gently in his arms to immerse her just enough so that she could perform the gestures she could not have made on solid ground, to give her strength and unblock her joints, stretch her muscles and tendons. It was an activity known as "aquatic physiotherapy," and Chris was one of the rare practitioners of this fairly recent method, although he had not invented it.

Axel had taken note of this detail at the hotel when requesting a nurse for his daily treatment. On the list the manager had handed him he saw Chris's name under the column "New: Aquatic Massage!"

"Yes," confirmed the manager, "he's a fellow who works as an instructor over at the Villa Socrates, you know, the centre for problem adolescents. As if there were any adolescents without problems, but anyway! I cannot recommend Chris too highly. Everyone is pleased with his work. Shall I make an appointment for you?"

"In the name of the hotel, please, not my own name."

Axel wanted to make the most of the encounter. If he trumpeted out his name, he would be identified at once; however, if Chris did not recognize him right away, the surprise would be all the more exquisite.

Axel studied him, making the most of Chris's extreme concentration in order to see without being seen. How kind he was! How good to that dinosaur with her wrinkled folds of skin . . . A stranger, on top of it . . . If the patient had been his own mother, could he have been any more tender, more considerate? Impossible. Bent over her worn face, manipulating her carcass like a dancer in love, looking deep into his partner's eyes, restoring the grace of movement to her. And what a physique . . . At the age of forty, suntanned, sharp crow's feet at the corners of his eyes, Chris had maintained the red mane of his youth, and hadn't put on one ounce of fat: his muscles were taut and prominent, his belly firm, with broad shoulders above a narrow waist, his torso finely sprinkled with hair as precisely as if it were make-up, shadowing his lower belly and emphasizing his chest muscles. Axel was all the more fascinated as he gazed at Chris because he could not help but compare himself to him. He envied above all his slender legs beneath his firm buttocks; Axel could no longer aspire to anything like that since his accident had left his thighs and buttocks paralyzed, and they had melted, atrophied.

"And whose fault was it?" he murmured with rage, rubbing his legs, stiff as iron bars, with his right hand.

Chris's athletic splendor merely reinforced his determination: no mercy.

Curled upon himself, his thoughts of revenge like a constant refrain, he was surprised when Chris touched his arm.

"It's your turn now, Monsieur."

Axel looked up anxiously. What if Chris recognized him right there and then?

"My name is Chris, and I'll be giving you a massage for an hour, that's right, isn't it?"

Axel nodded.

"What is your name, Monsieur?"

Axel uttered the first name that crossed his mind.

"Alban."

He bit his lips. What an idiotic thing to say! In the grip of their shared memory he had said "Alban," since it was Alban Berg's concerto "To the Memory of an Angel" that he had played in Chris's presence! Making such an obvious blunder— Alban!—meant that Chris would identify him instantly.

"Alban, I'm going to help you into the water. Allow me to push your chair, then I'll carry you over to the steps. All right?"

"Uh . . . all right."

Chris had not recognized him. Out of the corner of his eye, Axel understood why: in addition to the fact that Chris did not expect to see him, his behavior was ultra-professional: mindful never to betray shock or disgust in the presence of infirmity, for fear of humiliating his patient, he focused his attention on technical details such as removing the dressing gown, taking off the steel braces, grabbing his hips from the right side.

Reassured, Axel decided to relax and let himself go in Chris's arms.

Once they were in the water, Chris asked him if there were any contraindications, any movements to avoid. Axel shook his head. Chris then ordered him to close his eyes, and he began the therapy, explaining every movement with a calm voice.

This whispering in Axel's ear brought his confusion to a head. Ordinarily, when two people murmur, with their eyes closed and their bodies virtually naked, it is because they are in love. And yet here he was in the arms of his worst enemy, the man who, many years ago, through his arrogant carelessness, had nearly killed him. It was absurd . . . so very absurd . . .

Yet there was nothing painful about this troubling situation. On the contrary. With Chris's help, his body now lighter in the water, Axel felt as if he had been relieved of his infirmity. He was floating, turning, gliding. This unexpected, beneficial session took him back to sensations of childhood, to his first swims in a pool in Sydney with his father, his slender body against the immense, imposing adult one, then their expeditions into the deep waters of the Pacific at Whitehaven Beach, where he clung to his father as he made his powerful breaststroke: a little boy moved by this contact.

How strange it was to feel so trusting—their flesh touching—with his assassin . . . And what if revenge were to be reduced to this, to being manipulated by Chris, who would henceforth be his slave, every day until his last . . . At least it would be a form of torture—for the avenger as much as for his victim—that was out of the ordinary.

"Alban, how do you feel?"

Axel opened his eyes. Chris was rocking his patient in his arms, not eight inches from his face.

"Fine, just fine."

Their eyes met, and then Chris pointed to Axel's legs.

"What happened to you?"

"An accident, twenty years ago."

Chris shuddered. Not because he had guessed Axel's identity but because the time frame, twenty years, brought back certain memories. Axel hastened to distract his attention: "What gave you the idea to study this technique, aquatic physiotherapy?"

"Oh, I don't know . . . I wanted to come up with something good to do in the water."

"Why? Is it possible to do bad things in the water?"

Chris moved to the side to smile to a swimmer who was headed back to the showers and did not answer. Axel continued, "I had my accident in the water."

Chris turned around, and stared at him, numb, puzzled at first, then suspicious, then worried, then horrified. Axel held his gaze. He saw that Chris had realized what was happening; it was as if a curtain were being drawn open onto memory, allowing the light to enter progressively. He swallowed, then said in a toneless voice, "Is that you, Axel?"

"Yes."

Tears fell from his eyes. He was struggling not to smile.

"But then . . . you're alive?"

"What did you think?" exclaimed Axel.

In twenty years, Axel had never considered this hypothesis, for he assumed Chris knew what had happened after the drowning.

Chris suddenly looked down, as if he had just received a blow to the back of the head.

"I thought that . . . "

"Do I look like a corpse? I look more like an invalid, don't

I? I was re-animated when they brought me out of the water, I spent five months in a coma and when I came round I was nothing but a vegetable. I had to learn everything—no, relearn everything—how to speak, write, count, move around. As for my mind, I had lost nothing. However . . . "

He pointed to his shriveled right hand.

"No more violin."

He pointed to his feet.

"No more sports."

He pointed to his swimming trunks, his tadpole legs.

"No more sex. But, naturally, I'd hardly had time to even explore it very much."

Overwhelmed by his confessions, Chris suddenly found it difficult to touch Axel. He set him down carefully and respectfully on the steps to the swimming pool.

"Oh, I am so happy that you're alive, so happy!"

He looked closely at his wrecked body, his thinning hair, and he shivered: poor Axel, the neat, irreproachable face that was once his had disappeared, leaving behind a hard mask where his features, twisted to the left side of his face, no longer expressed feelings but only the fatal, flattened, ravaged consequences of an accident.

"Do you think that someday you will be able to forgive me?"

"What would that change?"

Axel's voice was hostile.

Chris paused to think, disconcerted.

Stubborn, feeling the fury boiling inside, Axel insisted: "What would that change? Would it give me back my body, my music, my lost years, if I forgave you?"

"No . . . "

"Ah, maybe it would change *your* fate. Yes, for you, no doubt, life would feel easier."

"No, I have been crushed forever by the burden of my guilt."

"So then what would it change? Answer me! Just answer me!"

Unable to control himself Axel had begun to shout, his metallic voice echoing under the humid vault of the swimming pool. The old man stopped whirling his arms about, and the chubby lifeguard leaned forward, ready to leave his chair to intervene.

Axel and Chris stared at each other for some time. Finally Chris said, "You're right. It wouldn't change anything."

"Ah . . . So, I won't forgive you. That's not why I came here."

Chris stared at him again. He realized that if Axel had indeed come on such a journey it must be for a precise purpose.

"What do you want?"

"Meet me at seven thirty this evening at the Grizzli restaurant, next to my hotel."

Back at the Villa Socrates, Chris went to spend a moment with Karim in the carpentry workshop. He chatted warmly with the adolescent, then went upstairs to dress for the evening.

He did not know what to expect from their appointment. Nor did he know what to think after that afternoon's revelation. The fact Axel was alive was excellent news, but it did not exonerate him, far from it: when he looked at this enraged invalid, with his rough voice and broken destiny, he felt as if death had merely been replaced by permanent torture. Would it not have been better if —

Horrendous! What he was imagining was horrendous. Once again he was fleeing his responsibility. What a coward . . .

It pained him to know that Axel, who had been betrayed, had not gone immediately to the great beyond. The only person who knew just how ugly Chris's crime had been had survived and been the repository of that knowledge for twenty years. And that is what Chris found so hard to bear . . . He despised himself.

At the restaurant Axel was waiting patiently, his wheelchair already in place at the table.

They ordered their dinner then began to speak.

While Chris kept his narrative to a minimum—his return, the sudden clarity that came to him, his decision to change the course of his life and take a different path, a path devoted to others—Axel told his story at length, with a multitude of details, first of all because it was something he had never shared with anyone, and then because he wanted to like himself that evening, and perhaps even be liked.

Chris discovered who Axel had become in the course of his successive stories. It was horrifying . . . Where was the angel he had known, the boy who dreamt only of art and music, the boy who was so well-acquainted with the sublime? Sitting there at table was no one but a cruel, unscrupulous business-man, who had no fear of illegality, from clandestine businesses to immoral ones, provided they filled his pockets; a man who sold toys containing toxic paint and scoffed at the fact that children had died, a man who cheated the state and exploited human misery, a magnate with an empty existence, loveless and friendless, devoid of any ideals. In brilliant form, Axel did not realize the effect he was producing; on the contrary, he was delighted with himself, and he thought he had Chris under his spell. Twenty years earlier Chris might have admired this ambitious rise to money and power, but the new Chris, a teacher for delinquent children, no longer cared for this sort of talk.

A misunderstanding arose between the two diners. Each one had kept the other alive in his imagination, picturing a strong personality with clear, well-defined features. Axel had become a standard of achievement for Chris, and Chris was a prototype of success for Axel. They had constructed their lives taking each other as a model, with the rather vague intention of supplanting that model and surpassing it. And now their imaginary constructs were in danger of collapsing.

During dessert Axel realized that his boasting had led to a hostile silence in his dinner partner. He in turn grasped the situation: each of them had changed, and now despised what the other had become. Their loathing was all the more violent in that Chris reminded Axel of the generous individual he had once been and would never be again, while Axel reminded Chris of how he had eradicated that side of himself that had once taken advantage of others.

They lapsed into a long silence, then with a sigh Chris felt obliged to ask, "Axel, why did you come here?"

"To offer you a deal."

"Right."

"From today on, you obey me."

"I . . . "

"That's what I'm asking as reparation. From today on, you will do everything I ask."

"But—"

"I'm not forcing you. You can refuse. In that case, I'll call one of my lawyers, they'll re-open the case, I'll inform them that I've found you and the trial will go ahead. You know as well as I do that there's no statute of limitations."

"Go ahead. Denounce me. I won't deny it. I am ready to pay for my crime, I've been expecting it ever since."

"Not so fast! If you pay for your crime in prison, you'll be paying a debt to society, not to me. What good does it do me if you're rotting behind bars? Justice will be done, to be sure, but I won't get anything from it. Don't you want to do me a favor?"

"Yes, Axel, I do want to do you a favor. I absolutely insist on doing you a favor."

"Then from today on, you will obey me."

"All right."

"Swear."

"I swear."

Axel ordered another bottle of champagne and filled their glasses.

"To us!"

"To us . . . " echoed Chris, hiding his stupor.

Axel drank his glass down in one gulp and immediately poured another one.

"Tomorrow you hand in your resignation. Bye-bye Villa Socrates. At midnight we'll be on the flight to Shanghai. Here, this is the address you can give people who want to stay in touch with you."

He shoved the business card into Chris's fingers, English on one side, Chinese on the other.

That night, when Chris went back to his room, he automatically switched on his stereo, and the concerto "To the Memory of an Angel" began to play. After a few notes, he collapsed on the bed. He felt like crying, yet he couldn't. He had taken a promising artist and disfigured him, turning him into a cruel, irascible tyrant, paranoid and unscrupulous. Without realizing it, he had done worse than kill an innocent boy, he had killed innocence itself. His victim had turned into a torturer. In the strains of Alban Berg Chris could hear his own story: it was not only a child who had died, but an angel as well. Nothing was left of the old Axel; evil had won. And devastation.

When do we become the person we are meant to become? In our youth, or later? As adolescents, whatever our gifts in the way of intelligence and temperament, we are shaped, for the most part, by our education, our milieu, and our parents; as adults, we create ourselves through the choices we make. If Chris had once been ambitious, opportunistic, and combative, it was because of the pressure his mother had put on him: she was a single mother who wanted her only son to succeed in her place. In order not to disappoint her affection, he had to be brilliant, wage war and triumph. His mother was convinced that if Chris's father had rejected her, it was because she hadn't been chic enough for him! With hindsight, Chris decided that his father was no more than a selfish, irresponsible man, an ordinary bastard. At the age of twenty, when Chris came back from Thailand, he had managed, fortunately, to curb his mother's pressure; his casual criminal behavior toward Axel had shown him that he was headed down the wrong path and so he had started all over, on the basis of new values. What Chris had not foreseen was that the opposite could also occur: a good man could become a filthy bastard. And while redemption may exist, so does damnation. And it is always voluntary. When an accident disrupts an individual's life, people react differently: Axel had enclosed himself in a cocoon of cynical disgust toward humanity, while Chris had opened himself, learning to love other people.

While Chris may have felt that he was now himself, did Axel have a similar feeling? How much did freedom have to do with it? And fate? Chris could not get to sleep, for all these dizzying thoughts.

Nor was Axel able to sleep. He went on the Internet to check that his business was all running smoothly. In his random browsing he read that millions of antidepressants were sold annually the world over, and this gave him an idea: he could create an elixir of St. Rita, supposed to fight depression. He would call it "Rita's Miraculous Water." Of all his various activities—toys, clothing, gadgets, pornography—it was his religious commerce that he found most entertaining. "Now that people no longer believe in God, they're prepared to believe anything! Astrology, numerology, New Age mumbo-jumbo, the rebirth of saints. Let's make the most of it." As Europe became less Christian, it did not become more rational for all that; superstition had merely increased and diversified. In the old days, Christianity used to offer a framework for belief, and now that there no longer was one, Axel could exploit the rich seams of people's credulousness. Why St. Rita and not some other saint? Because of an etching pinned on the wall in his room in Sydney when he was convalescing, learning to speak and write again: instead of appreciating that image of goodness, Axel had begun to despise it, just as he despised any of the ritual forms that goodness could take, and kindness along with it. One day he spat on the saint and decided he would side with the victors, and stay there.

The next morning Chris handed in his resignation to Montignault who, once he recovered from the surprise, told him he was sincerely sorry and would miss him. Chris went to see Karim and gave him his address in China, then he attended a last-minute party his colleagues organized to see him off.

"When are you leaving?"

"Tonight. For Shanghai."

Because they wanted to know more, he confessed he was going to look after a childhood friend who had settled there; he had serious health problems now, and had asked Chris for his help. As they listened to his explanation, his close colleagues recognized the Chris they knew, the defender of altruism, and they embraced him.

At seven P.M. Chris took his luggage and went to join Axel; he was checking out of the hotel and told Chris to get into a car.

The limousine drove around the lake and pulled up outside a luxurious hotel.

"Aren't we leaving from Geneva for Shanghai?" asked Chris, surprised.

"The day after tomorrow."

They spent two days in the luxury hotel; Chris never found out why. During their stay Axel ordered him to perform a number of insignificant tasks—to help him get up, wash, put his things away. Chris obeyed, just as he had promised he would. Nothing he did seemed to bother him in any way, particularly if it only meant taking Axel to the indoor pool every three hours for his treatment, although the consistency of Axel's body never failed to alarm him—his bones were so light, his movements so disjointed. Chris wondered if all the years to come were going to be like this . . .

There were telephone conversations he overheard, and he discovered that Axel always behaved like a boor—curt, tyrannical, insulting, scornful, unjust.

"Axel, have you done anything good—by that I mean kind—in the last few years?"

"Nothing. May the devil preserve me," laughed Axel.

"I will oblige you to."

When he had time off, Chris gazed at the Alpine countryside he would be leaving behind. It was something inexpressible, a mountain lake . . . Sometimes it was as if the water was filling an enormous hole, like a lid over an abyss; other times you saw the relief of the terrain as harmonious shores cradling a body of water. In short, the place where he had spent the last ten years seemed from one second to the next either terrifying or delightful.

At dusk on their last night in France, a taxi came to take their luggage to deliver it to the airport the next day. Then a Chinese man from Geneva showed up at the wheel of a black car. Chris did not understand a word of what he said to Axel, because they were speaking Mandarin; he merely noticed that the Asian man, as he scribbled Axel's instructions onto a sheet, was terrified.

They did not wait until dawn.

At five o'clock Axel ordered Chris to give him his shower, dress him, put him in his wheelchair and drive the car.

In the indecisive gray light of daybreak they left the hotel, went down toward the lake, and took the road along the shore, driving cautiously through the thick fog that clung to the banks.

"Stop, we'll park here," ordered Axel.

The Chinese man from the previous night stood stiffly by the side of the road, waving to them.

They left the car behind. In the stagnant air there drifted a musty smell of mulch and dead branches.

The Chinese man bowed and pointed to a low-lying wooden craft at the end of a dock made of ash-colored boards.

Following his orders, Chris helped Axel, as delicately as possible, to slide from his wheelchair into the boat; as soon as he was seated on the rear thwart the invalid pushed him away, exasperated.

Then they moved off, the throttle on low to keep as silent as possible. The Chinese man's silhouette at the water's edge thinned, melted, and faded away into the dawn mist.

"Where are we going?"

"You'll see."

Chris wondered: what was contained in the bags lying between them on the floor of the boat?

The farther the skiff moved from the shore, the deeper it went into the pea soup. In the middle of the lake, where the mist had erased the shores and the mountains in an icy world, Axel cut the motor.

"This is where the voyage ends."

"Here?"

"Here, in the middle of the lagoon."

With that word, Chris grasped at once what his companion had in mind. The opaque Alpine lake stood for the blue inlet under a Thai sun: Axel wanted Chris to know what it was like to drown. Instinctively, he leapt to his feet, ready to dive in to escape.

"Don't move!"

Axel had pulled a revolver from his pocket and was aiming it at Chris.

"I'm not joking," he insisted. "Sit down. If you don't do as I say I'll shoot."

Chris sat back down. He opened his mouth to try and bargain with him.

"Shut up! Today you're going to listen to me."

Despite his peremptory mannerisms, Axel was trembling. Was it from the cold, the emotion, fear, anger? There was not a nuance on his expressionless face, all muscles gone as a result of the coma; only his puckered mouth betrayed any tension.

"One day you chose a medal with the number one over me. Naturally, you may not have known that I might die as a result, but between winning and helping me you did not hesitate. This time you won't win. Open the bags."

The steel weapon glinted with flashes like lightning.

Chris leaned slowly toward the satchels. They were very heavy, and he dragged them closer across the floor. He opened them and found they were filled with lead weights tied together, with straps at either end.

"Fasten the straps around you."

Chris started to protest. The only answer he got was the barrel of the revolver against his forehead.

Chris reluctantly began to do as he was told.

"And do it properly! Make those knots more complicated, nothing that you could undo!"

Axel squeezed his finger against the trigger.

Over their heads a crow gave a shrill, desolate cry.

Suddenly Chris stopped stalling and set to work. Energetic and resolved, he applied himself. Axel noticed this, with some surprise, but made no comment.

"There," exclaimed Chris, "I have my ballast. What next?"

"Oh, you're in such a hurry . . . "

"There's no point hanging around, since I know how this is going to end. You want me to jump in the water or do you want to kill me right here?"

"Calm down. Anyone would think you're enjoying this."

"It seems necessary to me."

"Calm down, I said. We'll go at my pace. I'm the one who organized all this, not you."

"I disagree. I did too. Some of it. I'm responsible for what you became."

"A millionaire?" asked Axel with a burst of laughter.

"No, a murderer. Do you remember what Paul Brown, the American who was in charge of the music workshops, used to call us? The rivals, Cain and Abel. I was the bad one, Cain, and you were the good one, Abel. I was the one who was supposed to kill his brother. Which is what I did."

Axel stared at him, full of hatred.

"Ah, so you do feel guilty, after all?"

"Very. And now look: you're Cain and I'm Abel. It's stupid, no? In twenty years, we have swapped our roles. You are nothing but an explosive mix of suffering, exasperation and hatred. You were a prodigy and I've turned you into a monster. How could I be anything but ashamed?"

Axel aimed the gun at him, ready to fire.

"Shut up."

Chris went on, vehemently.

"I ruined you, Axel. You became the opposite of what you were. I knew an angel, and I've made you a demon."

"Shut up. I am responsible for what I have become. It's what I wanted: 'Never again,' I said to myself when I came out of the coma, 'I will never, ever, be a victim again.'"

"Strange. 'Never again,' is also what I promised myself when I got back to Paris: 'Never again, I will never be a murderer again.'"

They reflected for a moment on the irony of the fate which,

with a single event, had turned a bastard into an altruist and a saint into a crook.

The shifting fog, deep and light, a white obscurity, settled all around them, soundlessly, burying them beneath its thick muffling cloak.

Axel continued, pensively, "When I met you this week at the café, you were speaking to one of your hopeless adolescents about 'redemption.' I had not heard that word for years, or even thought about what it meant. You radiated so much conviction that I realized you must be speaking about yourself. After abandoning me like some old fish hook at the bottom of the lagoon you set about your redemption. That's when I understood that I had taken a road leading the other way; I was going down, while you were ascending. What is the opposite of redemption? Decadence? Damnation? Yes, it must be damnation . . . When I say that word, I am in pain, I feel like a victim all over again."

"You've got it wrong. Even if you may always be a victim of other people, you can avoid being a victim of your own self. It's in your power. It depends on you alone."

"I no longer have the strength, Chris. Once you become a cynic there is no going back, you have no ideals, you don't care about anything except pain. And ever since I found you the pain just won't go away, it's getting worse. Because the situation has changed . . . I used to hate you. Now I hate myself. I can see myself with your eyes, I can remember who I used to be, I compare. What do I have left, Chris, what do I have left?"

If he had removed his dark glasses, Chris would have seen that Axel's eyes were filled with tears.

He stood up.

"There is something I can do for you."

"No one can do anything for me."

"Yes. I can. I can help you become a good man again."

"Impossible. In the first place, I don't want to."

"I'll make you."

Chris reached out and took up the lead plates, looked into the fog to his right and jumped.

It all happened so quickly that Axel did not realize what was going on until he heard the splash of the body in the water.

Chris's head remained above water for a second, no more, the time it took for his muscles to try and resist and for his eyes to find Axel's. Then the weights took him to the bottom.

There were no bubbles. Chris must have been holding his breath instinctively.

Axel stared at the widening concentric circles until the lake became smooth again.

He mused that he ought to be satisfied. It was his will speaking the lines to him because in his inner self he felt nothing.

Suddenly air bubbles broke the surface; emerging from the depths the sound had a human resonance, as if it were coming from a person's mouth, expressing joy at being once again in a human element, of having escaped from a hostile environment.

The sensation was unbearable to Axel. He had just realized that his companion was in the throes of death.

"Chris!" he shouted.

His vibrant cry rose into the indifferent silence where the mountains slept. It faded. There was no answer.

Then, to rescue Chris, Axel flung himself into the water.

For years old Queraz, an occasional fisherman, a Savoyard with a face weathered by a life spent outdoors, would tell his eager listeners and any tourists who cared to listen a story that had been troubling him.

One morning when he was teasing the fish on the promontory by the road leading down from the Combaz chalet, a rocky overhang that can be useful on days when you don't feel like taking the boat out, he had witnessed an extraordinary scene. As was often the case in November, a thick shifting fog was dancing listlessly over the lake, veiling and unveiling the water in turn. For an instant old Queraz could see a boat in the distance; the engine was switched off, and two men were speaking, peacefully. Then the fog had shrouded the scene. He saw the boat again when one of the two men jumped into the water, carrying packets. A diver? The other shouted, sounded worried, then he too slipped into the lake. Two minutes later, when visibility returned, Queraz saw two heads on the surface, yes, it looked as if the second man had fished the first one out, but they'd drifted away from the boat. A sudden gust of wind spoiled the show. At least ten minutes of murk followed. Finally, when the air was clear once again, there was nothing there but the solitary boat in the middle of the water. Where were the men? At the bottom of the lake or on shore? Drowned, or safe? He thought he must have dreamt the scene.

After a week of thinking and hesitating old Queraz had a drink to give himself some courage and went to tell his story to the gendarmes.

"If anyone reports the disappearance of two people," answered the brigadier with a laugh, "we'll come and get you to tell your tale. Until then, go sleep on it."

Because of the telltale signs on his breath, the officers of the law had not paid attention to the illiterate man.

It had so annoyed old Queraz that from that day on he had begun to smoke dark unfiltered Gauloises and developed a habit for absinthe, the local Alpine spirit.

His brain was ruined by alcohol, and he was on the verge of forgetting the vision he'd had when another event came to remind him of it.

Ten years later, as it happened, when it had been decided to empty the lake in order to clean it up, two corpses were found. On a bed of silt two bodies lay intertwined, head to tail, like twins curled up in their mother's belly.

No one ever found out who they were. However, because the workers who discovered them were struck by the similarity of their skeletons, the stony promontory opposite the spot where they had come to die, and where old man Queraz had witnessed their ultimate attempt at salvation, came to be known as the rock of Cain and Abel.

LOVE AT THE
ELYSÉE PALACE

She had come home to flee the streets, but now no sooner was she between her four walls than she wanted to go out again. Her malaise was getting worse by the day: nowhere did she feel at ease.

She looked all around her for some detail— a painting, an object, a piece of furniture—that might reassure her, restore her confidence, connect her to her past. In vain. The apartment on the top floor of the palace was depressingly tasteful: everything, from the tiniest molding to the fabric on the chairs, had been designed by one of the very best contemporary interior architects; if you so much as moved an armchair or threw a colored sweater over the combination of beige and lemony wood, it would destroy the harmony; any trace of a different, personal life, oblivious to the artist's obsessions, would be blasphemous, a blatant obscenity. She felt like a perpetual stranger here, in this décor that was supposed to belong to her.

She did not want to turn on the lights, and she sat down on the sofa as if she were visiting.

It was a dreary day; only the gleaming silver boxes gave off any light. Outside, snow was falling indolently. You could hear cars in the street accelerating with a muffled roar.

Catherine mused that her life was like a Sunday afternoon—long, morose, full of indefinable hopes and vague regrets, where bitterness prevailed and prevented her from enjoying the little there was left to enjoy.

At a loose end, she picked up the magazine her private secretary had left for her. A portrait of herself and her husband was on the cover, with the headline, A PERFECT LOVE STORY.

She immersed herself in the magazine with a smile. Her face was elegant, fragile, as diaphanous as bisque porcelain.

"A Perfect Love Story . . . What imagination!"

With the tips of her fingers, nails painted the color of red currant jelly, the flamboyant tones of auto bodywork, Catherine leafed through France's most popular weekly magazine, a gossip rag that nobody bought, of course, but which, miraculously, everyone had read and where, now, photos of herself and her husband were splashed across several pages. Under each pose was a caption repeating the title of the article, A PERFECT LOVE STORY. Henri and herself smiling to the camera, holding hands, shoulder to shoulder, affable, smart, well-groomed, poised—or rather carefully posed in their impeccable presidential apartments.

"Do we make a handsome couple?" wondered Catherine.

She was at pains to answer; with an eye that had become professional after twenty-five years of political experience, she knew that the photographs were superb, but what about her and her husband? To be sure, their defects were well hidden by make-up, and touch-ups could emphasize their qualities, and both of them were wearing clothing that showed them to their best advantage. Yes, they had triumphed over the ravages of time, they were looking their best, and matched their own iconic selves; did they, however, make a handsome couple?

"Would I like this couple if I had just met them?"

It was difficult to reply. Once she managed to stop thinking about the fact that they were the ones being examined, she still saw a powerful twosome, a man and a woman who were a cut above other people. And this, oddly enough, displeased her. Despite her social ascension, somewhere inside her there was still the student from the École des Beaux-Arts who had chosen to be a nonconformist, who had chosen to take a degree that would lead nowhere, a wild young girl who preferred to eat pasta for months on end rather than remain under the yoke of her parents, the free woman who had met Henri in a bar near Assas, never thinking for a moment that their affair might last. Twenty-five years later the Bohemian student found herself handcuffed to glory, frozen in the role of an official personage, Madame Morel, first lady of France, wife of the president of the Republic, pinned inside the gilded frame of the Elysée Palace.

"Well, one thing is for sure: I would not want to spend any time with that woman on the photograph."

She condemned herself out of hand: suit made to measure out of a fine cloth of elegant simplicity; heels high but not too sexy; hairstyle as solid as a helmet; modest demeanor. She had become bourgeois. The metamorphosis had occurred gradually, against her will. In the beginning, Catherine didn't give too much thought to the clothes she wore, and willy-nilly she would pile on dresses, shirts, long skirts and Indian vests that were colorful and cheap and which she was in the habit of picking up for a song in the working-class neighborhood near the Gare du Nord where she rented a garret room; at the most, to justify her choices, she would have said she liked the dry feel of cotton in thin layers against her slender body. Then, on her husband's arm, as he rose through the ranks of power, her casual style had begun to attract attention: while her outfits may have been of no concern to her, people had begun to comment on her devil-may-care attitude. Her indifference to fashion was seen as clever, a deliberate PR strategy hatched in her husband's communications offices; when people spoke of Madame Morel, they would either begin or end their discussion with her wardrobe, sometimes to praise her, more often to make fun of her. To put an end to the sneering she had relented and begun to dress in a more conservative style, emptying her closets of her hippie rags to fill them with outfits designed for women of her age who were in positions of responsibility. A question of dignity . . .

"Dignity! You understand, my poor Catherine, you come across as a frump who's convinced she's dressing 'in a dignified way.' The morons have won the battle: they've contaminated your brain."

She looked more closely at the photograph of the cold hallway of the Elysée where she was shown greeting the German chancellor: she could not bear to see herself like that. To be sure, she was perfect, attractive and elegant, but how could she stand there smiling, playing the role so well, never revealing for an instant that she was ill at ease. They'd stuck her with a role she did not want, that of a politician's wife; she had started as the wife of a deputy, then of a deputy-mayor, then of a minister, and at each step she had lost a little bit more freedom; after a disastrous election she had become the wife of the leader of the opposition, and that had actually been rather amusing, the best period; finally, unfortunately, these last few years she had been thrust into the position of the president's wife.

"No one would believe me if I admitted that my life has been a failure."

She turned the pages of the feature and laughed when she saw the photograph showing them in the Salon Doré, poring rapturously over an art book; the journalist had written, "Madame Morel is trying to share her passion for contemporary painting with her pragmatic husband." Yes, the scribbler was right, she had tried for thirty seconds, one minute at the most, the time it took to take a photograph, no more; and what's more, she had said any old thing when she pointed to the reproductions: why couldn't she have said something intelligent, Henri wasn't listening, it was all staged, just a silent tableau in a crèche.

"And what about Henri? If I were meeting him today for the first time, what would I feel?"

This thought was more interesting than the previous ones. She scrutinized her husband on the glossy paper.

"Play the game, Catherine, erase your memories, pretend you don't know him."

She shivered: he made an impression on her.

Yes, he did make an impression on her, with his rogue's lips, his ironic eyebrows, his perfect teeth, his black hair as brilliant as a raven's wing, his powerful neck emerging from a blue suit with an irreproachable collar. How could this be? After twenty-five years of marriage, she trembled as she looked at his strong hands, as if they were made to encircle a woman's waist; how touching, that hooked, determined nose, which expressed his energy; she was overcome by the dark flame burning in his eyes. So, could she fall in love with this man if she met him today?

Catherine looked up and became lost in thought, her heart in an uproar, as she contemplated the snow-covered garden. Seagulls were crying, shrill and furious, over the frozen ponds of the Elysée Palace.

This revelation was disconcerting to her: was it good news, or bad?

Bad! It was so useful to think that everything had died since they'd become prisoners of their roles. Why wake up a statue? I don't know if, at the Musée Grévin, the wax figures would like to be restored to life, if Joan of Arc would like to roast again, or Louis XVI to feel the guillotine's blade, or if Juliet would look forward to a new fatal adventure with that idiot Romeo. No, you can't bring old dolls back to life, you have to let them get covered with dust, and fade, and be buried in oblivion, to quietly leave behind the memory of the living. That was how Catherine Morel had been intending to live for years. So it was not good news to find she desired the fifty-year-old that Monsieur Morel had become, and not just Henri, the young man with wild hair she'd once known, and who had been embalmed alive in a president's suit. Not good news at all.

And yet . . . If only it were true . . . If they could remove the glaze of routine . . . If they could burn for each other once again . . . If they were better suited to their roles . . .

Instinctively she headed toward Henri's room where, like Bluebeard's wife, she was not allowed to enter. In actual fact she went there often because his bathroom, during the day, remained a mysterious place, without him and yet full of him, with the lavender smell of his towel, his toothpaste, the cold water on marble, the aloe foam; mysterious with the drifting ghost of her man; mysterious because he never allowed her to go in there with him; mysterious because this corridor led to a place of pleasure, preceding the night, when bodies would be entwined in sheets. A vestibule to love . . .

She sighed. Unfortunately this den had not been leading to any pleasure for a long time now . . . For all they slept in the same bed, Henri and Catherine no longer touched one another. The wearing of time, again . . .

She went back into the drawing room, picked up the magazine, and inspected her husband on the photos.

"This man is attractive because I don't know him. For example, I assume he'll be just as forthright as his attitude suggests, as frank as his smile. Yet I know . . . it's too late . . . I know who he is, what he is capable of . . . I know that . . . "

At that very moment President Morel appeared, dressed in blue, flushed, perspiring, a tight smile on his lips.

"Ah, you're here?" he said, surprised, somewhat brusque. "I thought you were out shopping . . . "

"Sorry. Nothing tempting in the boutiques, I came home quickly."

He came closer, intrigued.

"Are you all right?"

Was he truly worried or was he pretending?

"I'm fine. I was reading this feature about us."

"It's a good one, no? Rigaud is very pleased with it."

"Well, if Rigaud is pleased . . . "

She would have liked to add, "If the President's director of communications is satisfied, then the President's trophy wife must keep quiet," but she refrained from voicing her thoughts.

"Everybody thought you were magnificent," he declared, heading for the bathroom.

"Who is 'everybody?' Did you order a survey? Organize a referendum?"

"Everybody means the men in my cabinet."

"And the women?"

"The same."

Behind the half-open door he rummaged in closets, swirled water, moved flasks around.

For a split second she felt like causing a scandal, suspecting he might be on his way to see his mistress; she couldn't care less about adultery, it was of no interest to her at all, because he'd been cheating on her for years, but she thought it was unfair, vulgar, scandalous that he behaved in this way, showering her with oozing flattery while he was getting ready to go and see another woman. She very nearly blurted, "Will you pay the same compliments to your tart as you did to me while you were dolling yourself up for her? If she's not a complete and utter slut, she'll be annoyed. As I am." But she merely added with a sigh, "Chores waiting?"

"A meeting at the University at Jussieu."

He used these official visits as a pretext, that she knew, to visit his mistresses beforehand; he was well-organized, and only his chauffeur and bodyguards, men he could trust, would help him indulge in his little misdeed; the car would be parked just outside the building while he dispatched his business; with his Pompadour he would have just enough time to come, but not to make her come. Basically, there was no reason why she should envy them, the busy man's adoring doormats . . .

She smiled and put on one of his favorite CDs.

Henri came out of the bathroom knotting his tie over a clean shirt.

"Goodbye then, Catherine, see you tonight."

"I doubt it. I'll be at the theatre. Schmitt's latest play."

"Oh really, is it important?"

"For people who like the theatre, yes; for everyone else, it doesn't even exist. Put your mind at rest: I'll be there for both of us. As usual, I'll make the sacrifice."

"You may complain, but you love the theatre."

With a jaunty air he came over and proffered his lips, like a busy man who takes the time to be tender. At that very moment she caught a whiff of his perfume. She stiffened. Where did that perfume come from? Who had given it to him? Who had chosen that unfamiliar fragrance? There could be no more doubt about it: he had a new mistress, a regular. Prostitutes don't give perfume, only a sentimental volunteer would have the nerve. While ordinarily Catherine would hide thoughts of this nature, she heard herself say, "Who gave you that perfume?"

"But—but, you yourself did."

"It wasn't me."

"Ah . . . I thought it was . . . "

"No."

"Well. I don't know . . . I didn't pay attention . . . I get so many gifts . . . Rigaud, maybe?"

"You have men choose your perfumes for you now?"

"Why not? You're not going to go and have a jealous fit over some perfume?"

"No, I'm not stupid: I have better reasons than perfume to have a jealous fit; in that department, I'm spoilt for choice."

He looked at her, on the alert, ready to go into battle, a political beast who could convince a bald man to let his hair grow.

She forestalled him by quietly saying, "I won't make a scandal. I don't feel jealous at all."

"Oh . . . good."

"Not one bit. I'm as calm as a millpond. It's strange though . . . Perhaps people are right when they say—even though it just seems like common sense—that jealousy is a proof of love?"

He shuddered, wounded. Poor President, she thought, amused, he's so used to flattery, and has been so over-protected, that now he's vulnerable: he's as vexed by a furtive remark as if he had slipped at the polling booth.

"I'm not sure I understand," he whispered.

He was insisting because, as a rule, he had nothing to fear from a discussion like this. Catherine had grown accustomed to keeping her recriminations to herself. She recalled this character trait and at that moment she decided that he really was too lucky, and for once she would go against the grain of his habits.

"You heard me, Henri. I don't love you anymore. Not at all."

The President suddenly looked like a little boy who's been caught and punished, who is hurt and disappointed, and who is trying to stand up to the hurt and behave like a man. To finish him off she added, "And this is nothing new!"

"Catherine, are you joking?"

"Do you find it funny?"

"No."

"So it's not a joke."

He stammered, choking with rage. As frightened as a rabbit caught in a car's headlights, overwhelmed by anxiety, he recoiled sharply, then wrinkled his nose, then his whole body began to tremble. All he could produce was an incoherent spluttering, and he was about to say something when Catherine interrupted:

"I assure you, Henri, you're not suffering. It's just your male pride that is wounded. And male pride counts for a great deal in who you are. How much? Let's say eighty, eighty-five percent of your personality? Fortunately in a few minutes your mistress—you know, the nose, the perfumer—will be there to console you."

He went pale, incapable of determining what shocked him the most, Catherine's words, or her tone—distant, amused, almost indifferent.

"And has it been a long time?"

"A long time what, Henri?"

"That . . . that you . . . that you no longer . . . What you just said."

"Oh, that I don't love you any more?"

She stood thinking.

"A very long time. I could say it has been since you no longer have a moment to spare for me, but that wouldn't be true, it started even earlier. I could say it has been since you started using our marriage to convince the French that you are a man just like them, but that wouldn't be true either, it was even earlier. I could say it has been since you started kissing me in public and never in private, but that wouldn't be true either, it was even earlier. I could tell you that it's been since you took your mistresses, but that wouldn't be true either, it was even earlier. I could tell you that it has been since you had the indecency to use our daughter's deafness to make public opinion feel sorry for us, but that wouldn't be true either, it was even earlier. The truth is, it has been since the time of the attack. The attack on the Rue Fourmillon."

He swayed, his lips trembling with rage. His voice echoed against the age-old paneling, cold and sharp: "What do you mean by that?"

"You heard me. I know."

"What do you know?"

Everyone in France remembered the attack on the Rue Fourmillon. According to political experts, if that year Henri received the votes that he had failed to get before, it was because he had been the victim of a despicable aggression. While he was on official business, two men in balaclavas had opened fired on the car. Henri had been wounded, yet he tried to run after them, then abandoned the chase to turn back to his driver, who was bathed in blood. Public opinion had praised his courage; by the very next day he had become a political hero; in forty-eight hours his detractors were taxed as extremists and fundamentalists, dangerous men capable of ordering an assassination. His opponents had been discredited by the affair, and Henri had won the presidential election hands down.

"I know, Henri dear, I know what some people suspected but didn't dare put in writing. I know what you will deny until the end of your days, firmly and indignantly. I know what you did: you conceived, organized and paid for the attack. It was a pure exercise in PR. Nicely thought out, too, because thanks to your plan, you became president. It is a pity that because of your ambition your former employee is now quadriplegic and glued to a wheelchair. I have had nothing but scorn for you since that day."

Silence put an ever greater distance between them. A cold hatred permeated the room.

"I think you're going mad," he said slowly.

She picked up the magazine and handed it to him.

"Now look! Since you know what I know, look! See what a great actress you live with . . . I know just how low you can go, but I'm smiling. I'm bored, but I smile. I am unhappy but I smile. I despise you but I smile. It's remarkable, isn't it? I don't look like a victim or a torturer. It's great acting, why don't you applaud? You ought to, because you're the only one who can gauge just how good my performance is. 'A Perfect Love Story'—your Rigaud has every reason to be pleased with this article: you've gotten off easy!"

"So it's war?" he asked.

"Not at all, it's our life."

Henri looked for something to say in reply, could not think of anything, and walked toward the door, stiff, starchy, and furious.

At the door he turned around and said, "Why are you coming out with all this today? Why this sudden fit of sincerity? Why now?"

She opened her eyes wide like the dials of a clock.

"Well, I really don't know. Truly."

"Oh, really," he grunted, skeptical.

"I swear, Henri. And on top of it I feel so relieved that I wonder why I waited so long."

He shrugged, went through the door, slammed it, and stormed down the stairs.

If he had not been beside himself with anger, he would have gone closer to Catherine's face and would have seen that for the last few minutes she had been crying.

The months that followed merely increased the tension between them.

From the outside, it seemed nothing had changed: the presidential couple continued to assume its responsibilities— receptions, visits, travel—which also meant miming their love for each other; not a single hurtful word was uttered, either in public or when they were alone.

But their silence did not calm them; on the contrary, it served to exaggerate beyond measure the fatal words that had been at the origin of their falling out; as for their impeccable behavior, oiled from years of practice, it became the curtain behind which their hostility grew and intensified.

Overwhelmed by surprise, Henri suffered more than Catherine did, and while like most prideful people he had no problem with the knowledge that he was disliked, he could not bear the idea that he was scorned, still less when the disdain was coming from the person closest to him, who knew him best of all. Three possible solutions sprang to mind: either he admitted Catherine was right, which meant conceding that he had indeed deceived his close collaborators and cheated in order to win; or he could try to justify himself to his wife; or he could deny everything outright. Naturally, he chose the last option. Relieving his conscience, never for a moment envisaging that his better half might be justified in her rebellion, he forgave himself and rewrote history: the problem no longer stemmed from Henri himself, Catherine had become the problem. He began to complain about the fact he had to put up with such a companion—she was crazy, schizoid, bitter, jealous of his success and successes. What a strange personality! She was false, two-faced, split in two, charming in appearance and hateful in reality, like Dr. Jekyll turning into Mr. Hyde.

As for Catherine, she found this new situation very amusing. She enjoyed tormenting her husband. At least she had left behind her decorative role as well as that of the helpless, deceived little wifey. He was afraid of her. Now she imposed the presence of an unpredictable woman on him, a stranger whom he dreaded, as could be seen by his forehead full of tics and his eyes with their black irises that seemed to be pleading anxiously: "What will she do next? What will she say? What is she thinking?" Catherine made it a point of honor to withhold any answers or clues; she gave him no purchase; better still, the more she slipped away from him, the more she forced him to look at her constantly, obsessively. She only got up on the stage of her life for Henri's sake. She had had millions of spectators for years now, in France and abroad, since her position placed her in the limelight of global attention, and yet until now she had only ever fascinated naïve boobies who assumed she was in love with Henri and happy to be the first lady. Since her confession she had gained a lucid spectator who appreciated her performance and could tell just how much she was expressing the opposite of what she felt; henceforth, not only did Henri realize, he was also horrified. How delightful . . . The President, however, like any politician worth his salt, knew that no one could simulate constant sincerity, that people lied, used cunning, made promises, and forgot; and, like all politicians he also believed up to a point what he was playing at: emotion, indignation, anger, determination, power, helplessness. Therefore to him Catherine's utter cynicism was like an abyss where only the damned moved restlessly about.

Henri hated this forced cohabitation with his wife. Then, through contamination, he began to hate Catherine herself.

He made less and less effort to hide his feelings. He removed the mask of the attentive husband the moment there were no more witnesses; no sooner had the couple settled into a car, no sooner did he return to the palace than irritation, hostility, and rage ravaged his features. He was filled with spite and bile, he boiled with suppressed rage.

Catherine could not get enough of this sudden violence—it was like a whip, bringing her to life, tearing her away from ennui; she delighted in it the way a tree delights in the sap rising in springtime. For while it may not have meant a revival of their love, it was certainly a revival of their story.

One day when she was wandering from boutique to boutique in Saint-Germain-des-Prés, escorted by two bodyguards and a chauffeur, she noticed off in the distance an individual in a beige mackintosh who crossed her field of vision several times.

She knew immediately what this meant: her husband was having her followed. She exulted. Not only did she pretend not to see the detective but she also distracted the attention of her bodyguards several times so that they wouldn't notice him either.

"What is Henri looking for? What does he want to know?"

After a month had gone by she discovered the reason why

she was being tailed: the president was compiling a list of his wife's friends, in order to send each of them an invitation to the Élysée Palace for a "casual breakfast" without Catherine, where he would cleverly try to worm information out of them. His guests may not have realized, but the former lawyer who was now head of state was able to gauge how close each of them was to Catherine, and how much admiration or hostility they felt for his own person, his overall purpose being to determine whether Catherine might have shared with a confidant the explosive secret she possessed.

She thought it was great fun when her friends related their visit. They had been intimidated, flattered, and manipulated, but had never guessed the true reason behind Henri's behavior: his security.

"If he's tailing me, it's for his sake, not mine. He's only interested in himself."

As the man in the mackintosh, or a pale replacement, continued to trail her, she decided to play a trick on them.

She asked a certain Charles, a friend of friends, an antique dealer on the Left Bank, to receive her in his bachelor flat. The handsome forty-year-old—tall, slim, elegant, and still youthful despite the strands of white that made his dark hair iridescent, was honored, and agreed enthusiastically. Every day from five to seven she went to his house with an ostentatious discretion. Together, behind closed curtains, they drank tea, conversed, laughed, and listened to music, in such a way that she did not even have to feign the contented expression she wore on her face on leaving his building—click, photograph . . . Would this suffice to arouse President Morel's suspicions?

After a week had gone by she could see in Henri's eyes that he had been informed. How could she tell? From the gleam of joy: he hoped he had nailed his wife, since he had caught her red-handed.

She went on for a second week with her eager visits.

Once his suspicions had been confirmed, Henri could hardly hide his jubilation. Catherine, on the other hand, hid hers very well.

The third week she delivered the coup de grâce: she waltzed around Paris on Charles's arm, going to restaurants and the theatre. Then, since the hoped-for reaction was somewhat slow in coming, she made a few clever phone calls, with the end result that the paparazzi took pictures of the two new friends without them knowing.

On Saturday morning a picture appeared in the worst weekly gossip rag, with this caption: "With a favorite like him, the first lady isn't likely to make the President jealous." And the journalist went on to emphasize the fact that the antique dealer was a well-known homosexual. Indeed, the moment anyone made inquiries about Charles, they would immediately discover that he had a pronounced and exclusive preference for men. Only the two spies in their mackintoshes—because they were stupid—and her husband—because he was too fond of women—had overlooked this detail and assumed that Catherine had taken Charles as her lover.

That very evening, at a gala held at the Elysée Palace in honor of the Russian president, Catherine put on a long gown and walked along the solemn corridors to join Henri, who was gloomy, as if he were cross with her for not cheating on him. Now she was secretly delighted, and sat down compliantly to her umpteenth state dinner, a dinner as starchy as an apprentice maître d', a dinner without a single crushed flower, without a single colorful word or animated gesture or original idea, a dinner of wax dolls set among high ceilings and monumental tapestries.

Once the reception was over and they were on their way back up to their apartments, the moment they were alone in the staircase Henri ventured to say:

"How can you stand the fact that I have mistresses?"

"I am delighted that other women are fulfilling a task I no longer have the stomach for."

He stopped and looked at her, closing his fist to stop himself from hitting her.

"Do you know that any other man would slap you for making such a remark?"

She shook her head, doubtful.

"That's as may be. But would I say it to another man?"

He stepped closer to her, threateningly.

"Why don't you leave me?"

"You'd be only too pleased."

"And what about you, wouldn't you be pleased?"

"My revenge consists in staying with you."

"And yet you would be free!"

"So would you. And then you would be capable, my dear Henri, of enjoying your freedom more than I would enjoy mine. So I prefer to deprive myself in order to deprive you. Through my sacrifice, I shall always be better than you."

She was sincere. Her aggressive impulse would keep her faithful to him, just as she had been since the beginning of his presidential mandate. A saint. Impossible to find fault with her. Never had any woman applied herself so devotedly to not betraying her husband: and while in days gone by it had been out of respect, now it was in order to humiliate him.

He added, "You are perverse."

"And that, my dear, is probably why we once fancied each other."

They entered their apartments. Henri locked the door. They did not say another word until morning.

The next day the sun was shining on the lawns of the Elysée Palace like a miraculous promise.

Contrary to his usual habit, Henri insisted on having breakfast with his wife, and ordered two trays to be brought up, which he himself set out in the dining room. Forgetting the tension of the night before, he turned to her with an amiable manner: "Catherine, in a year and a half, new elections will be held. I'm going to seek a second term."

"I thought as much."

"What is your opinion?"

"You are not sure to be reelected."

"I know that, and I'll fight."

"How? You can't possibly use your assassination trick again, can you."

He clenched his jaw. And grimaced: "I don't know what you're talking about."

"Of course you don't."

In silence, each of them became absorbed for a minute or more in the task at hand, that of covering buttered bread with jam without getting any on the table or on their fingers.

Then he continued, as if nothing had happened, "Before my second mandate, I suggest we get a separation."

"Why?"

"What do you think . . . "

"That would be taking a major political risk, my dear Henri."

"A divorced president? Times have changed!"

"The surprise of it would be a serious blow. Ever since there have been newspapers, radio, and television, everybody has believed in our perfect love. 'A Perfect Love Story,' that's our legend. If people were to find out it was not true, just a smokescreen, a load of rubbish, it would create mistrust among your supporters, and have an even worse impact on those who are undecided: has President Morel been lying to us? How much truth is there in what he tells us? Has he done such a good job, after all? Are his deeds and gestures not merely the product of his communications strategy?"

"I don't care. I've had enough."

"Of me?"

"Of you! Of us!"

"And I suppose there is a new mistress who is dreaming of shoving me out?"

"Not even."

"What then?"

"I cannot stand the way you look at me."

She burst out laughing.

"That's for sure: I see you as you are. And it's very ugly."

He grimaced, swallowed his saliva; then, placing his open palms down on the table to calm himself he concluded, "Would you consider my proposal?"

"I have considered it: I refuse."

"Why?"

"I have found my way. What options remained after I discovered I no longer loved you? To hate you. It suits me."

"Catherine, I can no longer stand to have you by my side."

"Well, you are going to have to get used to it. Let me sum up the situation. First of all, you will not seek a second term unless I agree."

"I beg your pardon?"

"I would have to keep my mouth shut, keep my dirty secrets to myself, and not go blabbing about the attack on the rue Fourmillon."

He made a movement with his body as if he had received a blow to the stomach. Certain that she had been heard, she continued, "Secondly, during this second term, I will be by your side. 'A Perfect Love Story,' don't forget!"

He took a swallow of coffee; his gaze above the coffee cup was murderous.

"Why are you putting me through this hell?" he asked.

"So that you will pay for what you have done. For what you have made of me, of our daughter, of your principles, of our life, of your former chauffeur."

"You're going stark raving mad, Catherine: you are not only my wife, you are divine justice."

"Exactly!"

She spun on her heels and left the room.

The following week there was an incident to which, initially, she hardly paid any attention. On the way to spend a weekend at the Institute for the Deaf and Hearing Impaired where her daughter was staying, in Cognin in the Alps, the chauffeur stopped to check the brakes after they had gone a few miles because they were not working properly. Something which the mechanic at the garage later confirmed. Catherine praised Martin for having realized in time: the hairpin turns would have been fatal.

Then ten days later, on her way home from the Opéra de Compiègne, where she had gone to see *Le Domino noir,* a forgotten minor work from the nineteenth century, there was an accident.

At one o'clock in the morning, in the deserted streets of Paris, the limousine with Martin at the wheel was approaching the Pont de l'Alma by way of the underground expressway along the river when a white car with blinding headlamps came up behind them. Disturbing and irrational, the car was tailgating so close that Martin had to accelerate. Suddenly another vehicle heading the wrong way came at them in a furious zigzag, forcing Martin to swerve. A split second later the presidential limousine crashed against the column.

To a resonant *bang* and the crunching of metal, Martin cried out in pain and Catherine, sitting in the back, felt her knee tear apart.

The emergency services—firemen, ambulances—arrived quickly and the occupants were extricated from the vehicle, crushed but conscious.

On her way to the hospital, Catherine realized soon enough

that she would pull through, as would her chauffeur. However, this hardly reassured her because now she had identified the true source of danger: Henri!

As the siren tore its way through the Paris night, Catherine realized the full horror of her situation: Henri had ordered to have her eliminated. Since he no longer wanted her by his side, either for his upcoming campaign or for what might become his second term, he no longer had any scruples.

As she was taken through the emergency entrance at La Pitié-Salpêtrière she gave a sigh, relieved to find herself in a public hospital and not a private clinic, where he could have taken her hostage and acted just as he liked.

The greatest trauma specialists examined her, gave her a shot, provided her with oxygen, took a blood sample, then informed her that they would operate on her leg without delay.

When Catherine came round, it was Henri's face that she saw leaning attentively over her.

He immediately smiled, took her hand, and caressed her temples. Groggy and terrified, she let him. He spoke to her, and she answered with a grunt; he used the opportunity to go off into a passionate monologue. During what seemed an endless time to her, he held forth like the ideal husband, in shock, affectionate, as if he had been afraid of losing her, as if in his eyes she still mattered, as if he still loved her. He confessed to her, shamelessly, that the fact of having her with him again in this state—so weak, having narrowly survived—enabled him to gauge how absurd these recent months of dark moods, petty squabbling and estrangement had been. As a pledge of sincerity, tears welled along his somewhat Asian eyelids. Mute, sheltering behind her pain, Catherine could not get over it: how could he lie to her in this way? Even she would not be capable of such a thing. Her assassin was making perfect use of all the expressions, thoughts, and feelings of a victim! What a performer . . . She let him finish his show because she had neither the strength nor the energy to react.

In the days that followed he continued his starring role as the adorable worried husband, whether they were alone or in the presence of witnesses who could only look on tenderly. However, as soon as she felt she had her nerves under control, she took the opportunity of a moment alone with him to ask, "Just how far are you prepared to go?"

"What do you mean, my darling?"

"Just how far would you go for the sake of power?"

"What are you talking about?"

"As far as killing your wife?"

"You had an accident."

"Two in the same week. It's strange, no? First the brakes gave way. Then a trap."

"You're jumping to conclusions. The investigation is under way, they will get to the bottom of it. When we find that reckless driver, we will drag him before the courts."

"You won't find him."

"And why not?"

"Because you can never track secret agents down. Or, if you can, their files are protected by state secret."

"I don't understand."

"Two accidents one right after the other putting your wife in mortal danger . . . You will say it was a coincidence, or the law of series, I suppose? Besides, the only question I have is regarding your intentions. Did you want me to die? If so, your Secret Service is worthless. Or did you just want to frighten me? If that is the case, they obey you well. Successful intimidation or failed assassination?"

"My poor dear, you are in a state of shock."

"That's it, you'll finish me off with a team of psychiatrists to claim that I'm off my rocker. My leg in a cast and the rest of me in a chemical straitjacket, will that be my minimum sentence?"

"Catherine, I thought that this horrible episode of suspicion and hatred that we have been going through was behind us."

"Who stands to gain from this crime? You do."

"There was no crime."

"A likely story!"

"Listen, Catherine, no matter how I dream and hope and try, harder than ever, we cannot get along. As soon as you are out of the hospital, we should take a good look at our problems and talk about them and find a solution."

"Divorce? Never! Never, you hear me, never! You will not extort a divorce from me."

As she had been shouting, he stood up in a panic, afraid that his secretary out in the corridor might have heard her say "divorce." Then he looked at her, with a gaze that combined fear and compassion, and said, "I'll come again tomorrow, Catherine, please put aside these foul suspicions and pull yourself together."

He left her abruptly.

Alone again, Catherine succumbed to panic. How could she get away from him? Here in the hospital she had nothing to fear, but the moment she got out, she would be exposed to new dangers, the target of the very secret services who obeyed the orders of her all too powerful husband.

As fear is a good incentive, she found a way. She immediately asked to see as many friends and acquaintances as possible during the three days remaining to her in the hospital. Her telephone calls bore fruit: forty or more people came to see her. Every time he visited, Henri found her surrounded by company. He thought she had had a change of heart and he was glad.

Finally, the night before her departure, at twilight, the president was able to have a quiet moment alone with her.

Catherine gave him a big smile.

"I'll be glad to get home, Henri, yes I'll be very glad."

"Well then, so much the better," he said, with obvious relief.

"Up to now I was afraid to leave the hospital because I knew it meant I would be in the hands of people who want to harm me. Now I am reassured."

"You seem to have left your paranoid delirium behind, I'm delighted. I was worried."

She saw that he seemed sincere. What a fabulous actor he was, too . . .

"Yes, I shall return to the Elysée without fear. You, on the other hand, will be afraid."

"I beg your pardon?"

"Afraid that something might happen to me."

"Naturally, I'm afraid something might happen to you, I've always been afraid something might happen to you, there's nothing new under the sun."

"No, you will be more afraid than before. Because these last few days I made use of my visits in order to take some precautions. As of tomorrow, if I am hurt, there will be a letter. A letter that for now is kept in a safe place, outside the country, far away from your spies and your armed henchmen. A letter where I tell the story of the attack on the Rue Fourmillon—or what I know about it, which means, a great deal—and the various accidents that have just occurred, with my own little theories regarding who was behind them. If anything were to happen to me, the moment my letter is revealed to the press you can be sure there will be a thorough investigation this time, a real one, an investigation that you will have no control over."

"You're crazy!"

"If anything happens to me, you are fucked."

They stared at each other with hatred. It was as intense as desire, as violent as love, and it reminded them of how important they had been to each other a long time ago, at the beginning of their relationship, with the sole difference being that their feelings now led them both to desire the other's death rather than a shared future.

The doctor came in, stopped and looked at the two tense individuals, thought he was interrupting a passionate declaration, and cleared his throat.

"Excuse me for disturbing you, Madame, Monsieur le Président."

Catherine immediately put a friendly smile on her face and said in a breezy manner, "Do come in, Professor Valencienne, do come in."

As he did not want to stay in the background, Henri also indulged in a few friendly courtesies. He congratulated the professor, then pulled up a chair so that he could join them beside the bed.

Embarrassed, hesitant, the doctor reluctantly drew closer.

"Well, Madame, Monsieur le Président, we ran certain tests when Madame was admitted to the emergency ward. As regards the shock and its aftereffects, I think that our service has covered a maximum. You will be able to go on with your life as before. However, during our exams, we discovered something else."

The President motioned to the physician to sit down. He refused once again and turned to Catherine.

"We have to discuss a more serious health problem, unfortunately. The blood tests have revealed the presence of a tumor."

"A tumor?"

"A tumor."

"Do you mean cancer?"

The professor nodded.

Catherine and Henri looked at each other with mixed feelings.

Henri stood up and said with an authority that demanded a frank and immediate response: "Is it serious, doctor?"

Professor Valencienne bit his lips, turned to look at the wall to his left, then the wall to his right, as if he were looking for inspiration and did not find it, and while looking at his white shoes he replied, "Worrying. Extremely worrying."

There were no better words for it.

The President let out his usual swearword, "Oh, shit"; as for Catherine, she fainted.

Catherine's health declined rapidly.

Once she was back at the Elysée Palace in their apartments under the eaves, for a while she went on hoping she would recover, although the exams showed that because the cancer had been diagnosed too late it was progressing at lightning speed.

Chemotherapy exhausted her. She lost her appetite. Her hair fell out. The specialists stopped focusing on the invasive metastases and decided to abandon any treatment. Catherine realized this meant she would not recover; she felt a strange sense of peace.

"So this has been my fate all along . . . I was bound to end up like this . . . and now . . . "

Contained within the fear of death, there are three distinct fears: we do not know when we will die, we do not know how we will die, and we do not know death itself. For Catherine, two of these factors had been clarified: she would die soon, from a generalized cancer. The anxiety that might now overcome her concerned only the actual state of death; and because ever since childhood she had been a believer, she did not dread the mystery of it; to be sure, she knew nothing about it—no more than the next person—but she had faith.

Henri insisted she remain by his side at the Elysée Palace, to be there for her friends who often came to visit.

They were all surprised, as was her husband, by her gentle docility. This tranquility came from the fact that she had interiorized her cancer. One day she questioned a young nurse who was giving her a shot of morphine: "If I had spoken sooner, if I had come out with what I had on my mind, could I have avoided the cancer? If I had freed myself through speech, perhaps the disease would not have taken hold inside me?"

"Cancer is an accident, Madame."

"No, it is a consequence. Sometimes cancer is the form taken by secrets that weigh too heavily."

Obviously, she did not claim to be right, but her point of view enabled her to accept, and to acknowledge that it was happening to her, and really to her, and only to her. Far from being an attack from outside, her cancer was becoming a story created by her body, her soul, her own self.

Rigaud, the President's director of communications, was lurking about. As she knew that he despised illness to such a degree that he had refused to enter the hospital where his own father lay dying, she concluded that it must be something other than compassion that had brought him there, so she asked him, over a cup of tea, to ease his conscience.

"I have something to ask you," he admitted. "The President was supposed to do it in my place, but he is so upset by the events that he doesn't dare. The fact is, may we make your condition known and announce your . . . difficulties . . . to the press?"

She looked him up and down, coldly. No sooner had she tamed her illness than he was plotting to take it away from her.

"Why?"

"The President will be embarking upon his campaign for reelection. And people are beginning to wonder about your absence. Some are saying that you are opposed to his new term; others maintain that you don't get along anymore; and still others claim that you are having an affair with a New York art dealer."

She could not keep from laughing.

"Oh, poor Charles . . . My Parisian antique dealer, now he's been transformed into a New York art dealer. And by crossing the Atlantic he's become a heterosexual! How well rumors do work . . . "

Rigaud went on, embarrassed: "Yes, Madame, we are hearing more and more rumors, each one more false and insidious than the next, and the President's grave expression only makes matters worse. So I have come to ask you to reveal the truth. You owe it to yourself, to the President, and to your exemplary marriage. Let us make all these dark shadows to disappear."

She thought for a moment.

"Will people be moved, Rigaud?"

"People adore you, Madame. You may expect numerous expressions of sympathy and sorrow. You will be submerged."

"No, what I meant was, will people be moved by Henri Morel, yet again, good, courageous Henri Morel, who survived an attempt on his life before his first election and who now before his reelection is nobly accompanying his wife's dying days."

"Well, it would seem that misfortune has not spared poor President Morel."

"Do you really believe what you are saying, Rigaud?"

He stared at her, intransigent, imperious, intense, and he chose not to lie: he fell silent.

With a nod of her head, she approved his silence, thus showing him that she was no fool, and that she knew a great many things . . .

A minute went by and neither of them moved.

"My answer is yes," she concluded.

An hour later, Henri, informed by Rigaud, rushed into their apartments to congratulate her warmly: "Thank you, Catherine. So you agree to let me run for a second term?"

"Is it in my power to stop you?"

He remained puzzled, wondering whether because of her

treatment and medication she had forgotten her threats. He went up to her gingerly and took her hand: "Can you tell me what you think?"

No, she could not. She no longer knew. Everything had become so confused. Tears stung her eyes.

Henri kissed her, held her for a long time in his arms, close to him, then when he felt she was relaxing and slipping into sleep, he let her rest.

Her illness had changed everything between them: aggressiveness would no longer be allowed access.

Catherine, in yielding to her tragic destiny, did not want to fight anymore; not only was it not in her nature but it reminded her of the weeks leading up to the discovery of her tumor; clearly she had been confusing irony, sarcasm, and verbal violence with the deterioration of her health!

Catherine consigned herself to silence, while Henri practiced conditional amnesia: he behaved "as if"—as if she had never expressed her disdain, as if she had never threatened to reveal what she knew about the attack on the Rue Fourmillon, as if she had not left a compromising testament somewhere abroad. He had been hiding these episodes so deliberately that he was beginning to wonder if they had ever taken place. He clung to his position as an ideal husband the way a drowning man clings to a lifebuoy, it was his salvation, the reality he wanted to manufacture. "The show must go on," he often murmured to himself, "Keep playing the part, show nothing of my inner turmoil or how worried I am."

And wasn't he right? Appearances could be a saving grace. When chaos threatened, only appearances could keep one from the edge of the abyss; appearances were very strong, they could hold, they could keep one from falling. "I mustn't fall," he said over and over, "I mustn't collapse, or give way to fear, not the fear of what she is going through, nor the fear of what she will inflict upon me."

They no longer knew what they thought. Either about themselves or about each other. The disaster had scattered onto the table the cards of a game whose rules they did not know; the illness, however, had brought both of them an unexpected wisdom: to live in the present moment, to know that they were ephemeral, to trust only what was temporary. Henceforth every morning they found themselves at the foot of a mountain, and they did not think about how hard the next day's climb might be. Although many details remained unresolved, they would take care of them when the time came, not before.

The media announced Catherine's illness and the news spread like wildfire. The radio, newspapers, and television spoke of nothing else for an entire week, for she was extremely popular, which meant respected and beloved. Catherine got the impression she was reading her funeral eulogy; from time to time a compliment would flatter her self-esteem; she often found herself pretty, even very pretty, on the old photographs they reproduced or the archival films the TV channels dug up, all the prettier for the way in which these recent weeks had taken their toll on her beauty. Whenever she caught herself in a moment of self-congratulation, at first she blushed, and then she forgave herself: after all, what other narcissistic pleasures were left to her?

However, when she discovered that the paparazzi were camping out in the neighboring streets or parking just across from the exit she always used at the end of the garden, La Porte du Coq, or even that they were climbing the walls to use their telephoto lenses to get their pictures of the mortally ill first lady, she summoned the President's director of communications.

"My dear Rigaud," she said, " these journalists will have to stop, otherwise they'll have no ammunition left for my death."

Rigaud swallowed his cake and promised that he would deflect their commentary onto the president.

And indeed, Morel's campaign, his dignity, his courage, the incredible strength which enabled him to wage so many battles monopolized people's attention. While as a rule politicians are shown grinning widely, Morel was increasingly photographed with pursed lips, a frown on his brow, and a dark look in his eyes.

As soon as he could, and far more often than she would have imagined, he came to join her for a silent moment or one where, in a brilliant monologue, he would share with her his confrontations, his plans, his intentions, and the disappointments of his adversaries. She listened to him with kindliness.

Finally there came the day when the doctor who was treating Catherine demanded that she be placed in a special home, better adapted to her weakening condition. Henri tried to protest and rebel; she merely nodded.

As soon as they were on their way, she wondered what his protestation meant: did he want to keep her by his side out of love, or was he afraid he could no longer control her if she were away from home?

They were driving to La Maison de Rita, a clinic located in the lush green countryside of the Loiret, a superb building set in the middle of an estate of centuries-old trees where, according to the publicity flier, there were thousands of bees.

The President went with her in the limousine to help her settle into this new home, and he grew indignant when he saw the name carved in fine gold letters above the entrance gate.

"La Maison de Rita! What sort of taste is that! To refer to Rita, patron saint of lost causes, to designate a medical facility!"

"Henri, I'm no fool," murmured Catherine. "I know it's a palliative care center for terminal patients."

"But—"

"I know I'll never leave again."

"Don't say that."

"Yes. So, La Maison de Rita suits me fine. Do you know Rita's story?"

As the car drove down the lane, gravel crunching beneath the tires, Henri looked at his wife in astonishment, wondering whether she wasn't making fun of him. As a precaution he answered in a neutral tone, "No, I'm not an expert in hagiography."

"Before she became an item for religious bazaars, Rita was a woman, a real woman, an Italian who lived in the fifteenth century and who managed to do something absolutely impossible: reconcile two families who had excellent reasons to hate each other: her husband's family, and the family of the murderer who had stabbed her husband. No one could match her when it came to attenuating hatred and pettiness, or exalting love and forgiveness. She suffered from a purulent wound on her forehead, but she managed all the same to live to a ripe old age, full of kindness, energy, and optimism, doing good all around her."

"You surprise me, Catherine."

"While you may not believe in the saints of the Catholic church, you still have to acknowledge that this *appellation contrôlée* is not awarded to evil individuals."

"True."

"Who knows what might happen in a house with such a name?" she added, rolling down the window and greedily breathing in the trembling leaves, the odor of the fresh earth beneath the plants, the beds of tulips bursting with health.

President Morel interpreted her words as a wish to recover and, full of pity for a dying woman who went on hoping, he thought it wise to break off the discussion.

Adjacent to a proud grove of oaks was a tall white building, half manor house, half château, with wide steps flanked on either side by sculpted lions, and doors bearing coats of arms. The director of the establishment, a blonde woman, was waiting for them by the entrance, her personnel standing on the steps in the manner that had once prevailed in châteaux, where all the servants lined up neatly to attend their master's return. Repeatedly she told the President and his first lady how "very honored" she was, conferring an atmosphere of official visit upon the sordid reality—so much so that Henri and Catherine winked at each other as she led them to a buffet of local produce with the pride of a woman who has just invented the petit-four, and they almost succumbed to uncontrollable laughter, something that had not happened to them for years.

Catherine was settled into a spacious room with windows that looked out onto the garden, then the President left to attend to his duties. He kissed Catherine on the forehead and promised he would be back soon.

For three days, despite his sincere desire, he was unable to find a moment to visit. His campaign was heating up, and he had to devote his time and energy to this new combat. But as he received updates every two hours, he learned that Catherine had requested a blank notebook and had started writing.

He realized what was happening.

"That's it, she's writing a confession in order to harm me. I have to go soon, and often, to see her. The less often I go, the more she will condemn me."

He was convinced that his presence would limit her venom, but for all that he did not manage to find the three hours in succession necessary for a visit, neither that day nor at any time during the three that followed.

On Sunday, it was a helicopter that took him to La Maison de Rita.

The obsequious director, dazzled by such a profusion of

means, led him, simpering, to his wife's room. When she opened the door, he gasped.

Sitting at her table, bent over her notebook, Catherine had changed; while throughout her lifetime she had been not so much beautiful as pretty, graced with a charming little face, now the disease had ravaged her, leaving her with shadows around her eyelids and a waxy complexion. Nevertheless, she wore a mask of great beauty, a slow, noble, priestly, expressionless beauty, more impressive than it was pleasing. And while he had not noticed anything when he could see her on a daily basis, Henri now realized how greatly she had been transformed. To some degree, this woman had already shed her mortal coil and left the world of the living behind.

"Hello, my dear."

She took several moments to react—everything was slower with her, now—then she turned around, saw Henri, and smiled. Her welcome seemed sincere to the President.

But as soon as he went over to her, she placed her hands on the pages she had just finished so that he would not see them, then closed the notebook and wedged it between her legs.

This reaction caused Henri to lose heart. So, he was right: she was taking her revenge.

For an hour he conversed with her, justifying his absence by telling her in detail and with humor everything he had had to do that week. In spite of her fatigue she listened attentively and although she could not laugh, during those moments when she normally would have burst out laughing she did screw up her eyes.

As he added one anecdote to the next he could still think of nothing but the notebook. Why didn't he have the guts to snatch it from her? Or at least talk to her about it?

Suddenly he pointed at it.

"Are you writing?"

Catherine's face lit up.

"And what are you writing, if you don't mind me asking?"

She hesitated, searching for her words, then she was pleased in advance with what she found to say.

"It's a secret."

He insisted gently, with no hostility: "A secret you can share with me?"

She seemed troubled, turned her head, and as she stared out into the garden at the setting sun she said slowly, "If I share it with you, it will no longer be a secret."

He swallowed his saliva and held back his irritation, then said confidently, "May I read it some day?"

There was a flash in Catherine's eyes. She pursed her lips, bitter.

"Yes."

The silence thickened. Outside, night was falling. The window was wide open and they could hear a golden oriole chirping and the sound of his beak against the bark. They were far away from everything, in the repose of a natural garden where the air radiated calm.

Henri did not turn on the light but allowed the darkness to fill the room. It was as if this twilight reflected their love: what had once been luminous had become cheerless and drab; the darkness was crushing them.

He kissed her on her forehead and left the room.

On Monday morning at 6 A.M., with the utmost discretion, he sent for one of the heads of the Secret Service, General Reynaud, and shared his concerns in the utmost confidence, exaggerating things somewhat: he was afraid that his wife, who was sick, and drugged, might write things that would be misinterpreted, or even used by his enemies. The general immediately sent someone to the institution to get hold of the incriminating pages.

Reassured, presidential candidate Morel returned to his duties.

In the weeks that followed he was swamped, constantly in

demand, rushing from meetings to television studios, and always ready to participate in stormy debates with his adversaries, so he did not manage, although he was racked by guilt, to visit her more than three times. With each visit he felt so bad that he behaved in an abrupt manner, and not tenderly enough; when he saw how much she had declined he became even more distraught. Although she did not seem to be offended, he knew he must annoy and irritate her, thus driving her to greater revenge in her writing.

The day of the election came. In the first round, Henri Morel obtained forty-four percent of the ballot, which was insufficient to win but augured well for a second round, because his opponents were divided and had no clear leader, as each one had garnered only ten percent of the votes. These scores encouraged Henri to believe that some of the voters would go over to him in the second round.

He pursued the battle energetically, particularly as the activity distracted him from Catherine's dying days and their imminent consequences.

On the Sunday of the second round, Henri Morel won the presidency with fifty-six percent of the votes: a landslide! At his headquarters they were exultant, his party rode a wave of jubilation, people rushed out into the streets to sing and dance and wave banners. He himself was obliged to drive down the Champs-Elysées, and to proclaim his gratitude from the open roof to the euphoric crowd.

Then he had to appear before the news cameras to comment on the election, and he strove to keep a grave expression on his face, for he did not want anyone to reproach him for his joy when the time came, any day now, for Catherine's funeral. To his surprise he realized, moreover, that he was so absorbed that he was not finding it difficult to maintain this dignified, introverted stance. During the night he celebrated his victory with the militant members of his party.

At dawn, all alone in his apartments at the Elysée Palace, he stood before the mirror and examined his naked self with neither sympathy nor complacency, and spent a few minutes analyzing the feelings that were troubling him: he did not want Catherine to die, for as many good reasons as bad. The good reasons were that he felt deep sorrow, stronger than he ever would have thought, to see his wife destroyed by illness. The bad reasons were that Catherine's death meant that the truth would come out, the revelations regarding the attack on the Rue Fourmillon and other damning details, an explosion that would have infinite repercussions and could easily destroy his political future, however officially glorious it might seem at the moment.

When he arrived that afternoon at the Maison de Rita, Catherine had just gone into a coma. According to the red-headed nurse at her bedside, she had watched the images of his reelection on her television the night before, and then she had wept, and fallen asleep. By morning she had lost consciousness.

A physician came to confirm that she would not wake up; the fatal outcome was expected within the next forty-eight hours.

Henri went onto automatic pilot, registering the terrible information with a nod of his head. He was so shocked that in fact he felt nothing.

Once he had listened to the director repeating ad nauseam, in her curt voice and with her empty administrative authority, what everyone had already told him, he took advantage of a moment alone with Catherine to search the room for her notebook.

In vain.

Exhausted, he could only hope that General Reynaud's agent had done the housekeeping before him. How could he be sure?

That evening in Paris, he organized a discreet meeting with

the general, who confessed that the agent whom he had planted in the kitchen at least a month earlier had not managed to get his hands on the notebook. Ordinarily, Catherine put it beneath her mattress, but this morning, after the news of her coma had spread, the man had not found it there.

Henri thought the ground would open beneath his feet.

The next day he went back to La Maison de Rita under the pretext of keeping vigil over Catherine, and at noon he created a scandal with the administration: where had his wife's log-book disappeared to? They were to deliver the notebook to him within the hour! A commando led by the servile director foraged everywhere for hours, searching the building and the staff's lockers from top to bottom, but failed to find anything. The president insisted on interrogating everyone: as a witness to the interviews, he realized soon enough that they would not find the slightest clue. After the last nurse had appeared before him, he thought he would fly off the handle; at that very moment the physician burst into the office to announce the death of his wife.

Catherine Morel was no longer of this earth.

From then on, Henri entered an icy corridor that he would not leave for weeks: he knew he was lost.

At the Elysée Palace he made the most of what people liked to call "his state of shock" to abstain from the organization of the funeral. Rigaud was very much at ease with this type of event, and he put together a lavish ceremony at Notre Dame Cathedral in Paris which was rebroadcast on a giant screen outside the building itself and to every television in every home in France.

Surrounded by the Garde Nationale, who added the brilliance of their helmets and the thoroughbred nervousness of their horses to the spectacle, the coffin was conveyed to the main entrance by a carriage laden with white roses; then it entered the nave, carried by young visual artists. Cardinal Steinmetz, a man of iron faith with a bronze voice, led the mass, with choirs, a solo performed by the most eminent diva, and symphonic interludes. Called to the altar, President Morel, with modest glasses on his nose, delivered a speech that he was supposed to have written but which was actually concocted by a brilliant humanities graduate who was employed at the Elysée Palace; for once no one reproached her for her lyricism or sentimental effusions. As he read the final paragraphs, very moved himself by the writer's sorrow, infected with the emotion that reigned under the cathedral vault, Henri could not hide from the thousands of tearful guests the fact that he was struggling to keep his dignity. When their daughter, who was deaf and dumb, came to pay tribute to her mother with a speech consisting of signs, grimaces, and gestures, even though no one understood a thing everyone was deeply moved, for she was so very expressive; it was considered the emotional high point of the funeral, this silent child silently addressing a silent coffin. There was a smattering of applause. Somewhat ashamed, his head bowed, Henri thought that Catherine would have despised this exhibitionist display.

A few hours later, once the earth had covered his wife's body, Henri began to think of the problems that lay ahead: the revelation of his manipulative behavior, the loss of his honor, lawsuits, the annulment of his election.

Although he sent the Secret Service in search of the diary, the investigation did not turn up a thing. No matter how the agents combed the homes of those who had been close to her, including Charles the antique dealer and their hearing impaired daughter, the notebook could not be found.

Henri Morel had not told either Rigaud or General Reynaud how much he feared the devastating contents of the manuscript. He had also hidden his marital conflict from them, the months of struggle that had preceded then accompanied her dying days. Like millions of people, they still believed in the "perfect love story."

One day General Reynaud asked to be received by the head of state.

Henri cleared his office of his advisers and welcomed him, feverishly.

"Well, General, do you have it? Do you have at last?"

"No, Monsieur le Président, but we have located it: it is in Canada."

"What is it doing there?"

"It is about to be printed by a publishing house."

"What?"

"I have consulted with the judicial experts: there is not a single loophole, everything is legal. The text was entrusted to the nurse who was looking after her, along with a letter signed by the late Madame la Présidente in the presence of a notary, who informed them of how to proceed, and validated each step of the way. The publication seems to be the execution of her last will and testament."

"We must contest it, we must claim that it's a fake!"

"That's impossible. Every document is in her handwriting. And the staff of the clinic saw her writing it for weeks."

Henri buried his head in his hands.

"The bitch thought of everything!"

Reynaud thought he must have been the victim of his own imagination: surely his dignified president could not have said such a thing about his beloved spouse. The old soldier coughed, blushed, and wriggled on his chair, ashamed that he had misunderstood.

"Thank you, Reynaud, thank you. Ask Rigaud to follow up and confirm your analysis. In other words, can we really no longer intervene . . . "

"I will see to it right away, Monsieur le Président."

He stood up and saluted. When he reached the door, the president stopped him: "Reynaud! What is the title of the book?"

"*The Man I Loved.*"

"*The Man I Loved?*"

"Yes. A fine title, don't you think, Monsieur le Président?"

Henri nodded to dismiss the general.

What an idiot! *The Man I Loved,* a fine title? No, it was evidence for the prosecution. It may as well have been *The Man I Loved and Who No Longer Exists* or *The Man I Loved and Whom I Was Wrong to Love.* It was a vitriolic title, it was poisoned, an apocalypse, and it was sending a clear message to the French nation: "The man whom you have wrongly loved, the man who you thought was dignified and honest and generous, is nothing better than a bastard," yes, what it meant was no more than *The Man Who Deceived You!*

"Rigaud!"

He shouted down the telephone. A few seconds later Rigaud burst breathlessly into the office.

"Rigaud, you must go to Canada. Deal with it as you see fit—steal it, pay for it, photocopy it, but bring me a copy of that book as quickly as you can. At once!"

Thirty-six hours later, Rigaud landed in Roissy, and climbed onto a moto-taxi in order to reduce the time spent going through Paris, then he rushed into the president's office.

"Here you are, sir, one copy of *The Man I Loved.*"

"And?"

"What?"

"You read it."

"I had no right, I had no instructions, you didn't want—"

"Rigaud, I know you! You read it! No?"

"Yes, Monsieur le Président."

"Well?" barked Henri.

Rigaud's face went purple, his nose twisted to the right, and to the left, then he said, looking away, "It is magnificent, Monsieur . . . Heartbreaking! The most beautiful declaration of love I have ever read."

From his pocket he pulled an enormous handkerchief, damp and rumpled.

"Excuse me, just thinking about it, it still makes me cry."

Crimson, he left the room, blowing his nose.

Disconcerted, intrigued, and worried, Henri grabbed the volume and opened it.

"At every moment, in this room where I have come to wait for my end, I feel an inner contentment, all the same. My heart is full, my soul is grateful: I met him. To be sure, I am going to die, but if I have lived, whether it was a little bit or a lot, it is thanks to him, to Henri. And to him alone.

"I often tremble when I think that I might never have gone into that Paris bistro in search of a cigarette, and I might have missed that Formica table where he was—already—rebuilding the world with his fellow students. The moment I saw him . . . "

Henri did not let go of the ribbon of sentences until the last word. When he closed the volume, not only was he sobbing like all those who in future would read the text some day, he was also transfigured: he had found his Catherine again, he adored her once again.

As she was dying, Catherine had composed a song of love—absolute, unprecedented, celebrating this man alone, the one who had enchanted her and filled her with enthusiasm and continually surprised her; the courageous, intelligent, and determined man whom she admired.

Our lives are such that the gaze we direct upon them can make them terrible or marvelous. Identical events can be interpreted as successes or catastrophes. And while, during their falling out, Catherine had interpreted their marriage as the story of a lie, she had since revisited it, during her last months on earth, and she had hunted down a great love.

Destinies are like holy books: it is the reading that gives them meaning. A closed book remains mute; it will only speak once it is opened; and the language it uses will be that of the person intensely reading it; it will be colored by his expectations, desires, aspirations, obsessions, violent impulses, and moments of distress. The facts are like sentences in the book, they have no meaning on their own, only the meaning that one gives to them. Catherine had been sincere in loving Henri, and sincere in despising him; each time, she had rearranged the past depending on what she had felt in the present. On the threshold of death it was love that once again had the upper hand; so the secret golden thread that had stitched the events of their life and gone on to become the thread of her writing was the thread of love.

One month after the book's triumphant publication, the nurse who had been in on Catherine's secret was summoned to a private interview with the president at the Elysée Palace. Although he acted very kindly toward her, or perhaps because he was acting so kindly, she asked him to forgive her: while she may have deceived him by not giving him the notebook he demanded at La Maison de Rita, she had been obeying Madame Morel's wishes.

"If you knew how much she idolized you, Monsieur! She waited for you from morning to night. She lived for you alone. Because she knew her end was near, she set herself two goals: to write this book, and not to interfere with your reelection. It was for your sake that she was able to hang on. That Sunday when she saw on television that you had won, she cried and said, 'That's good, he's won, now I can leave.' A few hours later she fell into a coma. It was her superhuman love that kept her going that long."

Henri Morel's final term in office, while it may have been the topic of much debate among political analysts—how could it have been otherwise?—provided everyone, including his toughest opponents, with an opportunity to admire the man.

Not only did he no longer have any mistresses, but he began to worship his late wife in a way that was all the more sincere for being discreet. Portraits of Catherine—photographs, paintings—invaded the president's private space, even his bathroom. With his own money and the support of a few benefactors he started a charity, the Catherine Morel Foundation, devoted to contemporary art, one of the deceased woman's passions, in order to encourage young artists by means of commissions, travel, and donations. At the same time the president seemed to be making up for lost time by reading the books she had recommended to him long ago. Every evening he would shut himself off in what used to be their shared living room and listen to some of her favorite music, light a room fragrance that she had chosen, and immerse himself in one of the books. And in those pages, even after her death, he could join her and try to continue—or begin?—a dialogue with her.

Pure souls, even abroad, were deeply moved by such unflinching devotion.

Are there any feelings that do not also harbor their opposite in their skin, like the lining of a fabric? Is there any love that is free of hatred? A hand that caresses may later pick up a dagger. Are there any exclusive passions that do not know fury? Are we not capable of killing with the same impulse that unites, the impulse through which one gives life? Our feelings are not protean but ambiguous, black or white depending on their impact, stretched taut between their contradictions, winding snakelike, capable of the worst as of the best.

Love had gone astray in the corridors of time. Catherine and Henri had begun by loving each other, then they had not known how to find each other, then they had appreciated each other only after the fact, one of them blazing with love while the other was full of hatred, and now death had abolished reality and its shortcomings. Memory enabled one to correct errors, to suppress misunderstandings and rebuild. Henceforth, for Henri, too, love had the upper hand. Sincerely.

When President Morel declined a third term and went into retirement, he married his past. Solitary, serene, smiling, the great man devoted his remaining years to writing his memoirs. For the first time in history the secrets of a head of state, while they did indeed describe his ambition and his political accomplishments, were simply entitled, in tribute to the woman he missed and whom he adored above all else, *A Perfect Love Story.*

I got into the habit, with the second edition of my books, of appending the writing journal that had accompanied them, and I subsequently discovered that my readers enjoyed reading what they found there. So for the first time I am adding these pages to an original edition. These are the passages from my diary that concerned the book as I worked on it.

Yesterday morning an idea came to me, so strong and seductive, so peremptory, that in forty-eight hours it actually took over my life, not the least bit embarrassed, changing my plans, the dispositions I'd made, and my questions, and it proceeded to make off with my future. It views me as a partner who must obey. The worst of it? That idea brought its family along with it.

Whereas for me it was enough merely to open the door: now I'm doomed, I no longer have any say in the matter: I have to write.

What was this idea? In his youth a man fails to come to someone's rescue. Through this act, the criminal discovers what a monster he is, then condemns himself and changes radically. Twenty years later, during which time he has become altruistic and generous, his victim finds him. But his victim has also changed radically: his suffering has left him spiteful, bitter, and cruel . . . The path each man has taken has reversed their positions: the victim has become the torturer, the murderer behaves like a good man. Redemption meets damnation . . . What will happen next?

As soon as I wrote it down, along came a cluster of new ideas. The theme of personal evolution through choice or traumatic experience has brought other stories in its wake.

This evening I've already had eight or nine ideas. My joy keeps me from feeling tired.

So one thing is certain: this is a book that is begging to be born.

*

Contrary to what many people think, a book of short stories is truly a book, with a theme and a form. While short stories may have an autonomy that allows them to be read separately, in my books they are part of a global project which has a beginning, a middle, and an end.

The idea for the book comes before the short stories, summoning and creating the stories in my imagination.

This is how I conceived *The Most Beautiful Book in the World* and *The Woman with the Bouquet.*

I don't make a bouquet by gathering scattered flowers, I choose my flowers depending on the bouquet.

*

Sometimes I write short stories for an event, a cause, a commemoration. These short stories are like loose sheets of paper. If one day I were to gather them together, I would call them *Collected Stories*, in order to distinguish this collection from the books conceived as a work in themselves. They will all fit in a volume, but will not constitute a volume.

*

"The Murderess . . . "

As usual, the character to whom I lend my pen has invaded me. Here I am, transformed into an old lady—something I'm used to—a provincial serial killer—something I'm less used to . . . How do the authors of crime novels manage to lead a normal life? I fear for my loved ones . . . Over the last few days I've become as vicious as my killer, I am no longer the least bit charitable, I kill people with my remarks, and it leaves me jubilant. In the kitchen, I see flasks not of oil or vinegar, but poison; I dream of horrible things while I season my sauces. Yesterday evening I was almost disappointed to be serving a mushroom fricassee which contained nothing dangerous.

Even when I'm not writing, my characters won't let me go. They haunt me, and sometimes even speak in my place. Their various roles fit perfectly, like a glove—but that doesn't matter—then they invade my mind. They mobilize everything inside me that resembles them. If the character is bad, then he or she exalts my nastiness.

I have already trembled, when I wrote *La Part de l'autre,* a novel about Hitler . . .

Tonight I was so upset that I thought that to get over this I might start on a biography of Saint Francis of Assisi . . .

Or Casanova?

*

These stories travel through existence wondering whether they are on the path of freedom or the road to determinism.

Are we free?

The question has endured better than its replies, and it will outlive every reply. For it seems dishonest, or cavalier, or stupid, to affirm anything with certainty.

We are under the impression we are free when we deliberate, hesitate, choose. But isn't that feeling an illusion? Didn't the decision have to be made no matter what? If our brain suggests an option, has it not been conditioned to suggest it? And what if it were a determining necessity, in the guise of free will . . .

Philosophers can choose to follow Descartes—freedom exists—or Spinoza—it does not exist—thus opposing each other yet never declaring a victor. Why? Because their blows consist of arguments, not proof. Theory against theory. With the end result that only the problem remains.

I confess I lean toward the partisans of freedom, like Kant

or Sartre, because I have the impression that in my life I have been able to experiment with my freedom. Moreover, I need to believe in freedom for moral reasons: neither ethics nor justice can be well-founded if man is not free, the author of his acts, and therefore responsible; nor can there be punishment or merit, either. Do we blame a stone for falling? Do we punish it? No.

However, if we need freedom for moral reasons, that does not constitute a knowledge that freedom exists. Postulating freedom is not the same as proving freedom exists.

The question remains.

This is the essential intimacy of the human condition: to live with more questions than answers.

*

This month, October, I'm on a tour of the United States and English-speaking Canada in order to promote the English translation of my first book of short stories. Originally entitled *Odette Toulemonde*, through the magic of translation it has become *The Most Beautiful Book in the World,* for the last story in the book, which must also be the most modest title in the world.

It has been well received. Imagine! This means that France is getting good press these days, because the reception granted to the very rare French books published in North America reflects the health of international relations. I find it amusing to learn that it is typically and almost exclusively French to want to mix anecdotes and philosophy, to speak about serious subjects with a mixture of lightness and depth. Today they applaud. On other occasions I have been faulted for that very thing . . .

During these literary festivals and the public readings where I am obliged to resort to the American translation, the listeners and readers' reactions are enchanting. They then rush over to the adjacent bookstore, where they are occasionally short on books, and they tell me they are fascinated by my sense of detail. And yet there is very little detail in my books . . . But it is through the use of detail that I tell the whole story. An old French tradition, where we say "the blade" for "the sword," or "the sail" for the boat. It's called synecdoche—using a part to describe the whole—and, beyond style, I apply synecdoche to playwriting as well, to the narrative process.

Indeed, the contamination of synecdoche is surprising in the Anglo-Saxon world, where so many systematically huge books are produced, loaded with detail and descriptions, the result of an immense labor of research and documentation, books where information streams in, hundreds of pages.

I think that the writer's art, like the cartoonist's, consists in making choices: choosing a proper frame and deciding which is the juiciest moment to say a great deal with a few words.

*

Still in America . . . I feel truly happy to be discovering books and authors that I did not know; I spend evenings with them over a drink remaking the world and rethinking literature, as if we were twenty years old . . . Their humble courtesy and respect for others are touching and inspiring.

This afternoon, in a packed auditorium, several American and Canadian writers gave readings, one after the other. Their texts were good, and yet I got the impression there was something lacking in the food, that it was the sort of nourishment that is not filling.

To be sure, when it's reduced to just a few pages, no excerpt from a novel could be self-sufficient, since it was meant to be part of an entire novel.

So it was easy for me to go up to the podium with an entire short story and delight the audience.

What is wonderful with Americans is their sense of fair play. My fellow writers, far from being jealous of my success, applauded warmly.

Here, too, I realized I had some lessons to learn . . .

*

In Toronto I chatted with a literary critic. All around us were piles of books, all mixed together, commercial novels with insane marketing campaigns, literary works, novels by sports or television stars who are not famous as writers but who write because they are famous, etc. A sort of nausea overcame me which I could not hide from him.

"How do you manage to sort through all these books, how do you tell them apart?" I ask.

"I count the dead."

"I beg your pardon?"

"I count the dead. More than two, it's a commercial book. One or two, it's literature. None at all, it's a book for children."

*

"The Return."

I wrote it far from home, like the sailor in my story. Going from one hotel room to another, I am tormented by nostalgia for my family. Impatient to be with them again, I have written this text for them so that, when I arrive home, they will, perhaps, understand how much I have missed them, how much I love them and, above all, how much I would like to love them better.

Work fills the hours, the measure of time becomes sentences that are never the same length.

If I could work on my life the way I write a short story, I might become a marvelous person . . .

*

I could never quite believe that Vancouver actually exists.

Located west of west, at the far end of an America that is itself at the far end of the ocean, this town has always been an abstract, speculative place, like infinity in mathematics. Vancouver seemed like a horizon which, like any horizon, would retreat as one drew nearer, the faraway West, the supreme West.

A faraway West even farther than the East since it was the dreams and determination of men that drove them to venture all that way. I found it hard therefore to imagine that there could be real streets, real people, stores, theatres, local newspapers.

Here I am on Grandville Island, a neighborhood known for its alternative culture, and I am standing opposite glass buildings where quick clouds pass.

I immediately liked the place. And I like the readers with all their different faces, books in themselves, because each one of them incarnates a novel, the story of how they came here, the story of their physique—Indian, Asian, Scandinavian, German, English—the story of their reconstructed lives.

I like Vancouver so much that I welcome it into my short story. It will be the homeland for "The Return."

*

Back in Europe, I am smoothing out the first two texts.

The other day I saw someone make a face at the mention of short stories, as if they were a sign the author was lazy or tired, and so I wondered why so little regard is given to this art form in France, despite Maupassant, Daudet, Flaubert, Colette, and Marcel Aymé.

Is it not a petty bourgeois sort of attitude to always prefer the novel to the short story? The same attitude that compels Monsieur and Madame Fromage to buy an oil painting for their living room rather than a drawing? "A drawing is smaller, you can't see it from a distance, and you never know whether it's finished."

I wonder if it isn't an expression of the bad taste of the affluent. They want their paint thickly layered, chapters with descriptions, dialogues with the consistency of chattering; they want historical information if the novel is situated in the past, or journalistic dossiers if it's set in the present day. In short, they like work, sweat, obvious skill, work you can see: they want to show the thing to their friends, to prove to them that they haven't been ripped off by the artist or the merchant.

"If you've got a novel of eight hundred pages," exclaims Madame Fromage, "you can be sure the author has put in the work."

But that's just it, maybe not . . .

To reduce a story to the essential, avoid useless adventures, pare a description back to a suggestion, remove the fat from the writing, exclude any complacency on the part of the author: it all takes time, it demands hours of analysis and critique.

In the end, if Monsieur and Madame Fromage deem the novel to be "more of an art form than the short story," it is because it is the quintessential bourgeois art.

*

As I reread the preceding paragraph, I realize that I have fallen into the trap of controversy: binary thought.

Here I am thinking just like those whom I reproach for shoddy thinking: I oppose, I dualize, I praise one at the expense of the other. How stupid! Thinking means accepting complexity, and yet controversy doesn't think, because it reduces what is complex to a duality.

In short, I love novels just as much as I love short stories, but for different reasons.

*

I have been awarded a prize in Italy for *The Woman with the Bouquet*, my second book of short stories. I get the impression that the critics there understand perfectly what I am trying to do because they know Italo Calvino's *Six Memos for the Next Millennium* by heart, and it is one of my bibles. They are not shocked if an intellectual seeks lightness and simplicity; on the contrary, they applaud because they know how truly difficult it is. With their Latin subtlety they do not confuse simplicity and simplistic.

Simplistic: ignoring complexity.

Simplicity: difficulties resolved.

*

I heard a lovely story in Verona.

In the first half of the twentieth century, a gardener was appointed to look after the cemetery containing Juliet's mausoleum. Tourists came to see her grave, lovers to kiss, and those who were sad, to cry. Moved by these scenes he witnessed on a daily basis, the gardener trained birds so that he could order them to go and land on the shoulders of those troubled souls and then give them a kiss, a furtive little peck with their beak. This was a pleasing phenomenon and gradually letters began to arrive from the world over to ask Juliet for advice in love.

The gardener got into the habit of replying, in his elegant style, and signing Juliet.

When he died, in the 1950s, the envelopes continued to pile up, at the address consisting of nothing more than, "Juliet, Verona, Italy." A number of Veronese decided to continue the practice and they founded the Juliet Club, a group of seven women who write letters in response to the unhappy or lonely hearts who contact them with their problems.

Yesterday evening I met the seven present-day Juliets—intellectuals, psychologists, sociologists, lawyers—who correspond with prisoners on death row in Texas or lighthouse keepers in China . . .

Strange Verona, built by the Italians and made famous by Shakespeare, an Englishman . . .

*

As usual, I have no life. My writing has taken over and put everything irrelevant on hold. I am now between parentheses, reduced to being a scribe, a hand in the service of an urgent impulse: characters who want to exist, a story that wants to find its words.

I go through the December holidays like a ghost. My obsession grants me a few hours of respite when I can have a sincere exchange with my parents, my sister, her husband, my nephews, and then as soon as I leave the room, the work in progress takes hold of me once again.

Sometimes I tell myself that writing does not like my family or my friends. Like an intransigent mistress, it isolates me, tears me away from them.

That is probably why I insert the people who are close to me into the writing process. I think about them, about how they will read me in the future, I try to surprise them, to amuse them, I make bets on what each of them will like or dislike on a given page. I insert them as potential readers of the text I am writing.

But as soon as I am sitting opposite them I am no longer there. I pretend to be myself and I remember that they are who they are.

*

A short story is the working drawing of a novel, a novel reduced to the essential.

It is a demanding genre, and does not forgive betrayal.

While a novel can be used as a junk room, this is impossible for a short story. The space granted to description, dialogue, or sequence must be measured. The slightest error of architecture will show through. As will complacency.

Sometimes I think that the reason I can blossom through the short story is because I am first and foremost a man of the theatre.

We have known ever since Chekhov, Pirandello, and Tennessee Williams that the short story form suits playwrights. Why? The short story writer has the feeling he is directing the reader: he grabs him by the first sentence to lead him to the last, without stopping, without a pause, just as he is accustomed to doing at the theatre.

Playwrights like the short story because they feel it restricts the readers' freedom, converting them into spectators who can no longer leave the theatre, unless they leave their seats for good. The short story restores this power to the writer, the power of governing time, creating a drama, expectancy, and surprises, pulling the strings of emotion and intelligence and then suddenly closing the curtain.

Its brevity places the short story on the same level as music or drama: an art of time. The time it takes to read—like that of listening or watching a spectacle—is regulated by the creator.

Brevity holds one captive to reading.

*

I am sensitive to one thing I don't often hear people discuss: the proper length of a book.

As a reader, I have found that most of the books I read are not the right length: this one might be three hundred pages whereas the subject only requires a hundred; that one is limited to one hundred and twenty when in fact it needs five hundred. Why has literary criticism consistently over-looked this criterion? As a rule it goes no further than point-ing out passages that are overlong, but only when it is bla-tantly obvious.

This lapse is all the more surprising in that, where the other arts are concerned, careful measures are taken to ensure the harmonious correspondence between content and form. In sculpture, people would generally be surprised if the artist were to chisel a monumental ensemble from a small stone, or shape a daisy from a granite block six meters high; in painting, the relation between frame, size, and subject are always respected; in music, one might consider this or that musical material to be insufficient for the length of this or that piece. In literature, never.

I am convinced that every story has its own density, requir-ing an appropriate writing format.

Many novels are little more than a recipe for some sort of swindle of a dish—skylark pâté for example: one part horse to one part skylark, in other words, more stuffing than pure sub-stance. Very often this is done to pad out a story, endless descriptions turning into a bailiff's inventory, dialogues that imitate life and destroy style, theories that are arbitrarily recy-cled, adventures multiplying like cancer.

When a New York publishing house brought out *Monsieur Ibrahim and the Flowers of the Koran* in the United States, one of the editors asked me whether I could not rewrite this eighty page novella and stretch it out to a minimum of three hundred and fifty pages, by filling out the stories of Madame Ibrahim, and Momo's parents and grandparents and schoolmates . . .

*

"Concerto to the Memory of an Angel."

I am writing it to the music of Alban Berg, which enchants me and procures unexpected sensations and new ideas.

For example, I had never noticed how much age can set us free. At twenty, we are the product of our education but at forty we are, at last, the result of our own choices—if we have made any.

The young man becomes the adult his childhood wanted him to become. Whereas the mature man is the child of that young man.

*

Can we change? And, above all, can we change voluntarily?

Here I am again, in the thick of these stories, confronted with the problem of freedom . . .

For the partisans of determinism, clearly man does not change, because he has no autonomy, no free will. Will is an illusion, and is only the name given to the most recent perceived conditioning. If an individual changes, it is from the effect of new coercive forces—social training—or a traumatic experience. Except in the case of an intimate wearing down of the machine, this comes from the outside . . .

For those who believe in freedom, the matter is more complicated. Is our will powerful enough to alter our temperament?

For certain people it is, those ambitious sorts whom I call the *partisans of sainthood.* Whether they are Jews, or Buddhists, or Christians, or even atheists like Sartre (who in *The Devil and the Good Lord* gives us a hero, Goetz, who alters radically from evil to good), they believe in our absolute power to achieve metamorphosis.

Then for others, the answer is no, for those cautious sorts whom I call the *repairmen.* Man does not change: he corrects himself. He uses his temperament in another way, he reorients it, places it at the service of other values. Chris, for example, the hero of "Concerto to the Memory of an Angel," grew up in a cult of competition, a dream of excellence, influenced by a mother who was unhappy and frustrated. After he nearly committed murder, in a state of shock, he preserved his character—energetic, combative, eager for success—but placed it at the service of good. He remains the same, even though the light he places upon himself is different: he has substituted an altruistic lightbulb for the individualistic one.

*

The force of will.

Without it, we would all have yielded to violent impulses. Who, when suddenly overcome by anger, fear, rage, has not desired, for a split second, to strike or even kill another person?

Sometimes I think that we are all murderers. The majority of humankind, the one which exerts self-control, is made up of imaginary murderers; the minority, of real assassins.

*

Marguerite Yourcenar said, "One does not change, one becomes deeper." Likewise, André Gide's advice was to follow one's path, provided it lay uphill.

When will connects with intelligence, man becomes an animal one can easily associate with.

*

Bruno and Yann have read "Concerto to the Memory of an

Angel." They come back to me, moved, and tell me I have written a beautiful love story.

I'm astonished. I hadn't realized.

*

"Love in the Elysée Palace."

When I'm working on this fable of love that is out of sync, I almost feel like I'm at the theatre. Henri and Catherine are strong characters, spectacular from the start. Virtuoso performers of appearance, they wear any number of masks, and have the richness of people who control themselves, and the suffering of those who keep silent.

At the same time, the story's setting can lay traps: the Elysée must remain in the background, power must be a mere framework justifying the fact that those who live there fear public opinion.

I was obliged to write the beginning several times to find the right angle, the one—a very simple one—that allows us to sympathize with an isolated woman who feels abandoned.

*

If this story, "Love in the Elysée Palace," is the final story in the book, it is because it holds the keys: like Henri and Catherine, people get lost in the corridors of time, they almost never experience the same feelings simultaneously, but they suffer from these painful time-lags.

Just as the murderess and her priest miss each other . . .

And Greg the sailor forgets to be a father when his children are still children.

And Chris and Axel are too different from each other to form a friendship; and when they change, it is symmetrically, which leaves them exactly the same distance apart . . .

When the day comes where explanations enable us to understand what we have missed, we find that those explanations still cannot repair the loss.

The redemption that flows from our realization often comes too late. Evil has been done . . . Making amends cannot undo what has been done. The daughters of Greg the ship's engineer will always suffer from the fact they were ignored and badly loved . . .

I could have called this book *The Time-lags of Love.*

*

Rita, the Madonna of lost causes, saint of the impossible, shines in these stories like a multifaceted diamond. Sometimes her brilliance is ironical, sometimes it triggers something, sometimes it is cynical, and sometimes hopeful. Its recurrence has the ambiguity of goodness: what appears good to one individual provokes the misfortune of another; what dooms Peter will save Paul.

Saint Rita tells no stories, but through her, stories are told.

This leitmotif is not meant to be an explanation on the part of the writer, myself, but rather a dig, a provocation, a mysterious kernel that will force the reader to think.

This morning I received letters from some German high school students who had studied *Monsieur Ibrahim and the Flowers of the Koran.* Amidst their compliments, one of them did complain: "Why don't you tell us why Monsieur Ibrahim keeps saying, 'I know what is in my Koran'?"

I answered him with one sentence:

"Because I want you to find out for yourself . . . "

*

Once a book is finished, its life begins.

As of this evening, I am no longer the author. The authors, henceforth, will be my readers . . .

Voltaire said that the best books are the ones that are half written by a reader's imagination.

I adhere to his idea, but deep inside, I always feel like adding, "provided the reader has some talent . . . "

*

To be precise: the idea that the reader may be more talented than I am doesn't bother me a bit. On the contrary . . .

ABOUT THE AUTHOR

Eric-Emmanuel Schmitt, playwright, novelist, and author of short stories, was awarded the French Academy's Grand Prix du Théâtre in 2001. He is one of Europe's most popular authors. His many novels and story collections include *The Most Beautiful Book in the World* (Europa Editions 2009) and *The Woman with the Bouquet* (Europa Editions 2010).

Europa Editions publishes in the USA and in the UK. Not all titles are available in both countries. Availability of individual titles is indicated in the following list.

Carmine Abate
Between Two Seas
"A moving portrayal of generational continuity."
—*Kirkus*
224 pp • $14.95 • 978-1-933372-40-2 • Territories: World

Salwa Al Neimi
The Proof of the Honey
"Al Neimi announces the end of a taboo in the Arab world: that of *sex!*"
—*Reuters*
144 pp • $15.00 • 978-1-933372-68-6 • Territories: World

Alberto Angela
A Day in the Life of Ancient Rome
"Fascinating and accessible."
—*Il Giornale*
392 pp • $16.00 • 978-1-933372-71-6 • Territories: USA & Canada

Muriel Barbery
The Elegance of the Hedgehog
"Gently satirical, exceptionally winning and inevitably bittersweet."
—Michael Dirda, *The Washington Post*
336 pp • $15.00 • 978-1-933372-60-0 • Territories: USA & Canada

Gourmet Rhapsody
"In the pages of this book, Barbery shows off her finest gift: lightness."
—*La Repubblica*
176 pp • $15.00 • 978-1-933372-95-2 • Territories: World (except UK, EU)

Stefano Benni
Margherita Dolce Vita
"A modern fable...hilarious social commentary."—*People*
240 pp • $14.95 • 978-1-933372-20-4 • Territories: World

Timeskipper
"Benni again unveils his Italian brand of magical realism."
—*Library Journal*
400 pp • $16.95 • 978-1-933372-44-0 • Territories: World

Romano Bilenchi
The Chill
120 pp • $15.00 • 978-1-933372-90-7 • Territories: World

Massimo Carlotto
The Goodbye Kiss
"A masterpiece of Italian noir."
—*Globe and Mail*
160 pp • $14.95 • 978-1-933372-05-1 • Territories: World

Death's Dark Abyss
"A remarkable study of corruption and redemption."
—*Kirkus* (starred review)
160 pp • $14.95 • 978-1-933372-18-1 • Territories: World

The Fugitive
"[Carlotto is] the reigning king of Mediterranean noir."
—*The Boston Phoenix*
176 pp • $14.95 • 978-1-933372-25-9 • Territories: World

(with Marco Videtta)
Poisonville
"The business world as described by Carlotto and Videtta
in *Poisonville* is frightening as hell."
—*La Repubblica*
224 pp • $15.00 • 978-1-933372-91-4 • Territories: World

Francisco Coloane
Tierra del Fuego
"Coloane is the Jack London of our times."—Alvaro Mutis
192 pp • $14.95 • 978-1-933372-63-1 • Territories: World

Giancarlo De Cataldo
The Father and the Foreigner
"A slim but touching noir novel from one of Italy's best writers
in the genre."—*Quaderni Noir*
144 pp • $15.00 • 978-1-933372-72-3 • Territories: World

Shashi Deshpande
The Dark Holds No Terrors
"[Deshpande is] an extremely talented storyteller."—*Hindustan Times*
272 pp • $15.00 • 978-1-933372-67-9 • Territories: USA

Helmut Dubiel
Deep in the Brain: Living with Parkinson's Disease
"A book that begs reflection."—*Die Zeit*
144 pp • $15.00 • 978-1-933372-70-9 • Territories: World

Steve Erickson
Zeroville
"A funny, disturbing, daring and demanding novel—Erickson's best."
—*The New York Times Book Review*
352 pp • $14.95 • 978-1-933372-39-6 • Territories: USA & Canada

Elena Ferrante
The Days of Abandonment
"The raging, torrential voice of [this] author is something rare."
—*The New York Times*
192 pp • $14.95 • 978-1-933372-00-6 • Territories: World

Troubling Love
"Ferrante's polished language belies the rawness of her imagery."
—*The New Yorker*
144 pp • $14.95 • 978-1-933372-16-7 • Territories: World

The Lost Daughter
"So refined, almost translucent."—*The Boston Globe*
144 pp • $14.95 • 978-1-933372-42-6 • Territories: World

Jane Gardam
Old Filth
"Old Filth belongs in the Dickensian pantheon of memorable characters."
—*The New York Times Book Review*
304 pp • $14.95 • 978-1-933372-13-6 • Territories: USA

The Queen of the Tambourine
"A truly superb and moving novel."—*The Boston Globe*
272 pp • $14.95 • 978-1-933372-36-5 • Territories: USA

The People on Privilege Hill
"Engrossing stories of hilarity and heartbreak."—*Seattle Times*
208 pp • $15.95 • 978-1-933372-56-3 • Territories: USA

The Man in the Wooden Hat
"Here is a writer who delivers the world we live in...with memorable and moving skill."—*The Boston Globe*
240 pp • $15.00 • 978-1-933372-89-1 • Territories: USA

Alicia Giménez-Bartlett
Dog Day
"Delicado and Garzón prove to be one of the more engaging sleuth teams to debut in a long time."—*The Washington Post*
320 pp • $14.95 • 978-1-933372-14-3 • Territories: USA & Canada

Prime Time Suspect
"A gripping police procedural."—*The Washington Post*
320 pp • $14.95 • 978-1-933372-31-0 • Territories: USA & Canada

Death Rites
"Petra is developing into a good cop, and her earnest efforts to assert her authority...are worth cheering."—*The New York Times*
304 pp • $16.95 • 978-1-933372-54-9 • Territories: USA & Canada

Katharina Hacker
The Have-Nots
"Hacker's prose soars."—*Publishers Weekly*
352 pp • $14.95 • 978-1-933372-41-9 • Territories: USA & Canada

Patrick Hamilton
Hangover Square
"Patrick Hamilton's novels are dark tunnels of misery, loneliness, deceit, and sexual obsession."—*New York Review of Books*
336 pp • $14.95 • 978-1-933372-06-8 • Territories: USA & Canada

James Hamilton-Paterson
Cooking with Fernet Branca
"Irresistible!"—*The Washington Post*
288 pp • $14.95 • 978-1-933372-01-3 • Territories: USA & Canada

Amazing Disgrace
"It's loads of fun, light and dazzling as a peacock feather."
—*New York Magazine*
352 pp • $14.95 • 978-1-933372-19-8 • Territories: USA & Canada

Rancid Pansies
"Campy comic saga about hack writer and self-styled 'culinary genius' Gerald Samper."—*Seattle Times*
288 pp • $15.95 • 978-1-933372-62-4 • Territories: USA & Canada

Seven-Tenths: The Sea and Its Thresholds
"The kind of book that, were he alive now, Shelley might have written."
—*Charles Spawson*
416 pp • $16.00 • 978-1-933372-69-3 • Territories: USA & Canada

Alfred Hayes
The Girl on the Via Flaminia
"Immensely readable."—*The New York Times*
164 pp • $14.95 • 978-1-933372-24-2 • Territories: World